ALSO BY ALISON RAGSDALE

The Art of Remembering

A Life Unexpected

Finding Heather

The Father-Daughter Club

Tuesday's Socks

THE LIAR AND OTHER STORIES

ALISON RAGSDALE

THE LIAR AND OTHER STORIES

This booking a work of fiction. Names, characters, organizations, places, events, and incidents either are products of the author's imagination or are used fictitiously.

For information: www.alisonragsdale.com

ISBN: 13:978-1-7330377-3-0

For all those who have little time to spare, but still need to lose themselves, one story at a time.

THE LIAR AND OTHER STORIES

A collection of short stories
by

Alison Ragsdale

1

THE LIAR

Verity had always hated her name. It felt like she had a mouthful of marbles when she said it out loud. Her grandmother had told her that it meant *truth* but that hadn't helped her like it any better. In fact, it made her feel small, especially as she'd become such an accomplished liar.

When she considered her life, she liked to think that she'd lied less to others than she had to herself. Regardless, the truth was often bitter, and every time she altered it, she thought about her grandmother and felt guilty.

Verity shivered then smashed her cigarette into the Mason jar full of sand, kept in the tool shed for the purpose. This was it, the last one. She was quitting. *Liar.* The packet she'd been hiding in the shed was now empty, and she was determined not to buy any more. *Liar.* She'd told her husband, Greg, that she'd given up two weeks ago. *Liar.* He was doing a good job of believing her, despite the faint smokiness to her hair, and the tinge of nicotine in her kisses. He wanted to believe her, so he did. That was the kind of man he was.

As she closed the shed door and walked across the damp

grass back to the dark farmhouse, she wondered if that was the trick to lying successfully. Perhaps telling someone something untrue, that they *wanted* to hear, made it a more legitimate practice, almost honest.

As she reached the back porch, Verity shivered as she tried to remember how long she'd been lying. Not little white ones, but big, dark, change-your-world type lies that stuck in her throat and threatened to choke her sometimes. She slid the kitchen door open silently, not wanting to wake Greg, and tiptoeing inside, she cast her mind back to her 8th birthday.

The last party her parents had allowed her to have had been a disaster. The cake, shaped into a perfect pink number eight, had been made by a neighbor and sat on the kitchen counter under a fine mesh tent. The sandwiches, cut into tiny crustless triangles, bled glorious strawberry jam onto her mother's best white serving plate, and several rows of cocktail sticks held together bite-sized chunks of cheddar, and pineapple, like golden kebabs. Bowls of potato chips and chocolate pretzels were pushed back behind the cake, and a tower of paper plates and napkins were stacked and ready.

Verity had been in her room crying for most of the morning. Her determination not to wear the fussy dress that her mother had picked out had led to her banishment from the preparations. After some time, she'd crept out of her room and lain at the top of the stairs and, with her head pressed up against the banister, she'd listened to the activity downstairs. Her three aunts had arrived to help, her father wisely staying in his study until his presence was absolutely required.

As fury at her isolation grew, so did the idea of how she could avoid wearing the dreaded dress. Her cat, Isobel, lay in a tight ball on the bed, and as Verity gently closed her bedroom door on the sound of her aunts' laughter, the plan blossomed.

Taking the gauzy dress from the hanger, Verity had sat on the edge of the bed and draped it over her knee. Isobel had such wonderful claws, so tiny and white and sharp. Verity loved to gently squeeze her paws, to see the little needles emerge, as if by magic.

Lifting one small, ginger foot, Verity had applied just the right amount of pressure. There, the perfect means to an end appeared. Isobel had stretched languorously, her back arching as she clawed at the bedspread with her other feet. Verity had carefully positioned the unknowing paw over the dress and dragged it across the flimsy fabric. The claws did their job, pulling several long strands from the skirt. She'd repeated the exercise several times, simultaneously rubbing Isobel's stomach, the result, a wondrous shredding of her floral nemesis.

The cat purred contentedly at the attention, as Verity, feeling only slightly nauseous at what she was doing, had spoken to her in gentle tones.

Mission accomplished, she'd hung the dress back on the hanger and draped it over the low chair in the corner. Carefully arranging the skirt to showcase the damage, Verity had pulled on her shorts and a T-shirt and gone downstairs.

Her mother had met her with raised eyebrows. "Who said you could come down, young lady?"

Verity had hung her head. "Sorry, Mum." *Liar.* "I'll wear the dress." *Liar.* She'd scrunched up her face, her regret a well-rehearsed mask, and then buried it in her mother's apron.

"All right then. No more of that. It's your birthday." Her mother had patted her back. "Let's go and get you dressed, then you can come and help me with the table."

At this, Verity had hugged her mother's waist, then turned and bounded up the stairs. Her mother had followed close behind, calling instructions to her husband, who had yet to emerge from his study.

As her mother came in behind her, Verity had been standing with her hands on her hips, surveying the damaged dress.

"Look what Isobel did, Mum." She'd pointed a treacherous finger at the torn fabric then, widening her eyes, turned and stared at her mother.

"Oh my God." Her mother was on her knees, lifting the shredded skirt from the chair. "It's ruined."

Verity had sniffed cleverly and walked over to the bed, where Isobel lay in innocence.

"Isobel, you bad cat. What have you done?" *Liar.* She'd shrieked at the animal and grabbed it up off the bed.

Holding the alarmed creature out toward her mother, she'd offered her little friend up in sacrifice. Her mother had stood, frozen to the spot, holding the spoiled dress in her hand, the torn fabric dangling down toward the carpet in floral rivulets. Verity had thought her mum's eyes looked weird, like they were looking at her but not seeing her properly. The cat had dangled awkwardly between them and begun to squirm in Verity's grip.

"Mum?" Verity had stood her ground and waited.

Several moments went by, her mother stationary, Verity holding both the wriggling cat and her indignant pose. Suddenly her mother's eyes had snapped back on.

"Give her to me." Her voice quiet and dangerous, her mother had tucked the dress under her arm and reached for Isobel.

"What will you do to her?" Verity, suddenly struck with the sickening realization that this could indeed be Isobel's end, had felt her throat narrow with guilt.

Her mother had turned and looked at her squarely. "Nothing." She tucked Isobel into her side. "But you will wear the dress Verity, just as it is." The words had been cold, not sounding like her mother at all.

"But Mum." Verity had been aghast.

"Do you hear me?" Her mother had stood in the doorway, a look on her face such as Verity had never seen before. "Just as it is."

The dress was flung back into the room and landed in a messy pile on the floor.

"I'll call you when you can come down." The door had closed sharply.

Furious that her plan had backfired, Verity had kicked the dress around the room several times, then wiped the hot tears from her dishonest cheeks. Opening the door, she'd stomped to the top of the stairs noticing that all was quiet. She'd strained to hear what was going on, but the only sounds floating up the stair had been the low rumblings of her father's voice and then forced whispering in response.

Grabbing the banister in her clammy hands, she'd leaned over and taken a deep breath.

"Mum." She'd yelled. "Mum." There had been no response. As the tears flowed freely, she'd tried one last time. "Muuuuuum. It was the cat." *Liar.*

"Verity? Is that you?" Greg's voice snapped her back to the chill of the dark kitchen.

"Yes." She gulped, huffing into her cupped palm, and then sniffing it.

"Were you smoking out there?" He walked into the room, his hair sticking up in the trademark cone at the back, and his bare feet protruding from under his pajama bottoms.

She shook her head in the darkness. "No. I told you I'd given up." *Liar, liar liar!*

R iver is an unlikely name for a dog, but that's where we found him. That Sunday morning was the second anniversary of us losing sweet Max, our fourteen-year-old Doberman, and as had become our habit on that date, Mark and I had walked Max's favorite route, the three miles out from Stanhope Point, toward the bay.

We'd planned on cutting through Buckhurst Woods, and then getting a coffee at the Bean Shack, before making our way home, but for some reason, we decide to add on an extra mile along the river and then cross back into town at the covered bridge.

We walked, talked about our boy, blew on our hands, faces pink, feet and legs tingling with the cold. The thought of a roaring fire at home was tantalizing so we picked up our pace as we approached the South side of the river, and that's when we saw him.

"What the heck is that?" Mark stopped in his tracks. "Looks like an old rug." He pointed at a dark mound heaped at the water's edge.

As we inched closer, the mound shifted, startling us to a

standstill. The rug was, in fact, a bedraggled mess of matted hair—all feet, and ears, and scrubby tail. Reeds were entwined in his fur. Burrs and twigs stuck out at crazy angles from his back and sides, making him look like a walking bonfire, but underneath the matted dreadlocks that were draped over the huge head, shone two bright eyes, amber-colored and wise.

As we both eased toward him, carefully, nervously talking in low voices, his tail twitched against the pile of brush he was lying in. A sign that we weren't wholly unwelcome.

"Easy, Lisa." Mark held his arm out, halting my progress. "It's an unknown entity." His military-esque speak brought a half-smile to my face.

As we got closer, the dog slowly raised himself up. Huge paddle-like paws spread wide, each toe elongating as it clawed deeper into the ground—his back lengthening in a theatrical stretch.

The water level was high that day. A ribbon of dark grey —the river rippled and folded angrily below the bank. It was bitterly cold, so we could see both our breath, and the dog's rising in smoky spurts, as we all panted out our anxiety.

It was obvious that the creature was pitifully underweight for his giant frame—perhaps only 45 pounds. He had no collar that we could see, so we guessed he was a stray, rather than a runaway. His appearance spoke to the length of time he'd been alone, his hip bones sharp through his skin, his ribs like a pair of matching xylophones, each one warped around either side of his torso.

"Hey, fella." Mark had half a granola bar stashed in his pocket that he held out, at arms-length. "Hungry?"

"Careful, Mark." I sidestepped to get a better view.

Crouching down, Mark crawled the last few feet toward the dog while I stayed back, not wanting to overwhelm him.

Mark crooned as he slunk forward. "It's O.K, boy. You look hungry. Here, have this. It's good." He waved the granola bar back and forth.

The dog locked him in a stare, his nose twitching almost imperceptibly as the granola bar entered his air space.

Mark slowed his movements. "Go ahead. Take it."

The dog stretched its neck out toward the food as Mark held steady. Its dark brown snout made gentle contact with the honey-soaked oat bar, and then, gingerly, almost elegantly, it drew the morsel into its mouth.

Mark turned to look at me, triumphant, a huge grin on his face. "See? He's harmless."

As Mark swiveled back around, the dog made its move. In an instant it was up and had crossed the narrow gap between them. Before we could react, Mark was on his back, pinned to the cold ground, with a massive paw planted on each shoulder.

I stood rooted to the spot, not sure whether I should shout, wave my arms, or try to drag the animal off.

Mark lay still, his head in some damp leaves, and his feet splayed out against the riverbank, with the dog's back legs planted firmly on either side of his hips. He lifted a hand to me, indicating that I should stay back.

The dog watched me, its head still, its amber eyes scanning my face.

"O.K., dog. You need to back off now." Mark's voice was low, steady.

The long filthy tail swished, first slowly then gradually faster as I took a step toward them and lowered myself to my knees.

"Hello." I moved slowly and kept my hands open in front of my body, low and visible.

The tail swished faster.

"Lisa. Take it easy." Mark twisted his head to look back at me.

"It's all right," I said. "He's calm." I continued to shimmy forward until I could reach out and touch the dog's matted side. "Hi, there," I whispered. "You're a handsome guy, under all that muck."

He assessed me for a moment or two, then lowered his head and licked the back of my hand.

"Oh, he licked me." I felt my throat narrowing. "Mark, he's so gentle."

Mark nodded, easing himself out from under the filthy paws. "Seems like it."

River came home with us that day, and now, six years later, we all walk along the river each Sunday and pay homage to the place that brought us together. He entered our lives when we needed him, a force of nature, an undeniable and inevitable presence that now we could not do without. He barged into our hearts so quickly, wearing us down with his mischief and simple adoration. Even if we'd had doubts about taking home a filthy stray, they didn't last, as nothing can resist the force of water for long.

3

THE HEDONIST

The ground came up and smashed into Amber's right cheek. Confetti fluttered away from her mouth as the last breath escaped her, and she felt the coldness of the hard concrete beneath her satin-clad hip.

As the chilly sensation slowly faded from her bones, so did the pressure of the unyielding ground, and she felt a strong vacuum suck her up into the atmosphere. She saw herself, many feet below, lying in a fetal position where she had slumped to the ground outside the church. The mother-of-pearl colored dress, she had searched for, for months, lay in a perfect semicircle around her. Her slim ankles protruded from the soft folds of the skirt, like the hands on a clock showing exactly six-twenty on the ground.

She hovered high above herself and looked down on the heads of her family, as they crowded around her limp form, shaking her, patting her face. Their voices were far away, distant, and yet oddly clear.

"Amber, sweetheart?" Her mother.

"Amber, honey?" Will, her husband of fewer than ten minutes.

"Oh God, can you hear me, Ambs?" Her maid of honor, and best friend of nineteen years, Louise.

"Call an ambulance, someone. Do it now." Father Brightman, the family priest, his white cassock pooling around his knees as he knelt at her side.

She wanted to tell them that she could hear them all, that she was here, but her voice caught in her throat, silent.

Is this it? Amber floated above these people she loved as a gentle breeze ruffled her hair, and, on a reflex, her hand went up to her head. She couldn't feel her hair under her fingers, but she knew it was there.

The version of herself on the ground remained still. *So, this was it then.* She felt a momentary flash of anger at the irony of it all, and then, a wave of warmth overtook her, a supportive bubble of calm settled beneath her, and she let herself be cradled.

It had been a beautiful ceremony with just a small group of people, important to both her and Will. They'd written their vows, but not the schmaltzy 'You're my best friend forever' kind of vows, more the 'I promise to tell you the truth, not to finish the ice cream without you, and never to ask you why you need to leave, as long as you come back' kind of vows. Will had given her a ring and, because it had been important to him, she'd agreed to wear it, despite her belief that she didn't need any symbols to seal her commitment to him.

Amber watched her parents far below. Her mother wept as her father folded his tailcoat and pushed it gently beneath his daughter's head.

She had struggled against their parenting, and opinions, for most of her life. Her teen years had been particularly difficult, especially when, at fifteen, she had run away. She'd taken a dead-end job in a sad, seaside town, and waited two months to contact them. She'd made them suffer, then, and looking down on the crowns of their heads below, she was doing it again, now.

Sadness overtook her as she realized that she couldn't even give them this special day, without a tiny artery in her head popping, and a searing pain behind her left eye sending her tumbling to the ground, in a heap of mother-of-pearl. She wondered if this was the final disappointment she could deliver. She wondered if she'd ever been the daughter they deserved.

Her mom had criticized her heavily, for many of her choices as a young woman: her blue-tipped hair in high school, her decision to take a year out to travel through Europe before college, then dropping out to pursue painting through an apprenticeship, and also for the way she moved between relationships, with a seemingly dispassionate attitude to the ones she was leaving behind. Her mother had tearfully called her behavior hedonistic, accusing her of putting the pursuit of pleasure before all other, loftier ambitions that *they* held for her, things they knew she was capable of.

Contrary to her mother's belief, Amber knew that she had chosen the path she was on because she was pursuing something more profound than pleasure. Happiness.

Will had allowed her the freedom she craved, without agenda or expectation, both in her work as an artist and in her constant need to travel. He called her his favorite nomad and would sit on the end of the bed and talk to her while she packed for her next adventure. She loved him for letting her go, to be who she was, with no guilt or emotional accounting. Eventually, after years of peripatetic work in several cities, from Florence to Santa Fe, she had realized that her heart just didn't beat properly when she was away from him. That had been why she had finally decided, after five years of his asking, to marry him, today, in the small stone church she'd attended as a child.

But now, thanks to that tiny artery, there would be no more happy reunions with him after yet another road trip to an artist's colony; no more laconic vacations, no more Thanksgivings or Christmases with her parents, no children to run around the yard or draw pictures for their grandparents' refrigerator. Perhaps she *had* deprived them all of those things with her choices? She had procrastinated like a pro when pressured by her parents to settle down, get a *real* job, grow up. Time and again, when cornered, she'd packed a bag and walked away, leaving them frustrated and asking themselves what they had done wrong.

There was no denying it, and as she watched her new husband and family circulating around her non-responsive body on the ground, she knew she had left them behind for the last time. Perhaps her mother was right, as, after all, this probably was the ultimate hedonistic act—moving toward her own bliss, not bound by the earth or other people's needs or expectations of her.

Amber filled her lungs with sweet air and felt herself moving with the gentle breeze. She knew she had to go but wanted to touch Will one more time so, willing herself closer to him, she moved down toward the ground, swimming through the atmosphere until she was behind him.

The back of his freshly cut hair tipped his shirt collar, and as he knelt, now cradling her upper body in his arms, she felt him rocking her. She reached out to place her hand on his face, but her hand was no more than a whisper of light.

I'm sorry, Will. I'm so sorry.

4

THE PIT

The dripping was driving Duncan to distraction. Moisture oozed from the coalface around them, and tiny black tears clung to the walls, dribbling down into several puddles on the floor. Some of the icy droplets splattered his leg, but he was too cold and exhausted to move. He could hear Sam's tight controlled breaths next to him, and Frank, groaning from across the dark void where he lay, propped against the dank wall.

They knew Frank had been hurt by falling rock but had no idea how badly. His breathing was raspy, and, once the dust had settled, they'd propped his head, as best they could, against a coal sack to keep him upright.

The oil-wick lamp Sam had been carrying, the only one that had survived the cave-in had run out a few hours earlier, and the single candle that kept them from total darkness sputtered and gasped for oxygen, as did the three trapped men. With only two inches of wax left to burn, they all stared with the same intensity at their remaining light source. If it could just last until they heard the digging of their rescuers it would keep them grounded, for a few more hours, providing a visual anchor in this dark hole. Without voicing it, they each tried to believe that soon they'd hear the sound of salvation. All hoping for the same deliverance, the silent prayers that surrounded the three friends were almost tangible.

Frank let out a low growl. In response, Duncan shifted his weight and made to get up. As his leg moved, and he slid slightly against the rubble beneath him, a soft cloud of dust rose around them. Nothing more than a puff, it was still enough to endanger the flame, which flickered ominously.

"Stop," Sam whispered. "Stop moving."

"I need to check on Frank," Duncan spoke out of the corner of his mouth, his eyes never leaving the flame, which gradually re-gathered momentum and then stabilized in its mission.

"Just take it easy." Duncan turned his head slowly to see Sam's eyes, stark white against the filth of his face, the coal dust thick on his skin. The eyes were full of warning, and he saw the fear that reflected his own.

Duncan lowered his hands to the ground, and very slowly, pulling his legs underneath him, raised himself up to his knees. Moving his weight backward, away from the candle, he maneuvered himself up to a stooped stand, as upright as the heavy anthracite ceiling would allow, and moved like a canny predator seeking to go unnoticed in the undergrowth, gently feeling each step out with his toe before transferring his weight forward in the darkness.

Frank was still. Duncan could just make out his outline, faint against the coal wall behind him. His head has dropped to his shoulder, and his arms lay motionless at his sides, palms up as if asking for the blessing of the great collier god.

Crouching down, Duncan put a hand on his friend's shoulder. Gently pressing his fingers into the rough-hewn shirt, he felt tackiness under his grip. Inhaling sharply, Duncan increased the pressure, willing Frank to respond.

"Frank. Can you hear me, pal?" He kept his voice low.

Frank groaned, and relief rushed up Duncan's chest.

"Where does it hurt, Frank? I can't see you very well." Duncan swallowed, his throat full of emotion. He hunkered down as close to Sam as he could, given the shelf of rock overhead, and the piles of rubble surrounding their feet.

"My shoulder, and my gut." Frank's voice was reed-like, and he gasped as Duncan released his grip. As he settled on the ground next to Frank, he reached over and searched for Duncan's hand in the darkness.

"Don't leave me here, Dunc."

Duncan shook his head. "Not ever. They'll be here for us soon. Just hang on a bit longer."

Raising his gaze, Duncan searched for Sam in the gloom. Lit from below, by the soft light of the single flame, Sam's ghoulish face was motionless in the tiny pool of light.

Duncan had always known that this could happen, all the years he'd been down the pit. There had been two cave-ins since he'd started in 1903, at fourteen years of age, but both times they'd been able to get those teams out within a day.

The brushers took enormous risks, going ahead to install the props and shore up the tunnel walls, making sure it was safe for the colliers to come in after them, with their picks. They all knew the risks, but figured it was worth the extra few coins it brought in at the end of the week.

By his reckoning, they'd been down here well over fourteen hours. He'd kept track of the time by checking the old strapless watch that lay heavy in his pocket. His wife, Sadie, made him take it with him to work every day, despite his protests that he didn't need a watch down the mine.

"You never know when you might need it." She'd patted

his pocket and smiled her crooked little smile, as he'd left the house that morning. He'd laughed and reminded her that they sounded a klaxon when the shift was over, so he'd hardly miss clocking-off time. Nevertheless, she'd insisted, and had checked again that he had it with him as she packed his lunch bucket.

Thinking about the way she greeted him every evening by throwing her arms around his filthy neck, then wetting her thumb and gently wiping the coal smudges from his cheeks, made Duncan's throat narrow. He'd roll his eyes and bat her off as she laughed in the musical way that had first caught his attention at a dance, twenty-four years ago. Now, crouched in the darkness beneath the weight of the earth above him, Duncan was overcome with wanting to hear that laugh, and feel Sadie's sweet, comforting breath against his cheek.

Fighting a surge of fear, he pulled the watch out of his pocket for the umpteenth time. Screwing up his face, as he held it up to his good eye, he tried to see the slim golden hands, working against the white background, indicating how much closer they had moved either toward their fate or to the end of this nightmare.

Sam's head suddenly snapped over his shoulder. "Listen."

His voice was sharp, and Duncan, lowering the watch, halted mid-motion, like a picture frozen in a frame.

Frank groaned.

"Shhhh, mate. I think I can hear something." Sam's face turned back to the candle's glimmering pool of light, and his eyes were wide.

Duncan strained to hear what Sam was referring to, realizing that Frank's breathing was so quiet he couldn't hear it anymore. Just then, there was a scraping sound. Duncan looked down at Frank to see if he had moved, but he was still, his head lolling over his chest.

"There it is again." Sam lifted his gaze to Duncan's, excitement creeping into his voice.

Duncan heard it now, a scratching, and tapping sound, coming from behind Sam's back. Making his way slowly back toward his friend, Duncan saw a small cloud of dust coming from the pile of rubble blocking the tunnel. A few particles of coal fell in toward them, and Sam, rising carefully, moved away from the candle toward the outer wall.

A larger piece of rock fell into their cave, followed by another then, as the candle finally sputtered out, a shaft of light broke through the pile of coal, as clouds of black dust rose around them.

"We're here, lads." Their foreman's voice crept in through the crack and wrapped itself around their frayed nerves. "Hang on. We're here".

"We're all right. There's three of us." Sam slapped his leg and shouted into the crack, stepping from foot to booted foot.

"Who's in there?" The foreman yelled over the metallic sound of shovels hitting the stone.

""It's me, Sam, with Duncan and Frank," Sam replied, turning to look at Duncan.

Duncan gave him the thumbs up as, slowly, the streak of light that crept in, from the now crumbling pile of coal that had imprisoned them, filtered toward the back of the cave.

Frank still sat as Duncan had left him, his head drooping over his chest. Duncan inhaled a deep, gritty breath, and moved back to his friend's side.

"Frank? They're here pal, we're O.K." He turned and beckoned to Sam, but Sam was intent on watching the diggers.

Kneeling next to him, Duncan reached for Frank's hand and felt the clammy skin under his fingers. With the increasing light, Duncan could see that the dark stain had spread from Frank's shoulder down the front of his shirt and that his hair was also matted with blood.

""Frank. Wake up. We're saved." Duncan shook his friend, but there was no response, and, just as he began to feel his throat closing in despair, Frank finally groaned.

"Jesus, you scared me there," Duncan exhaled.

Frank lifted his head, and his eyes searched for some reference to his surroundings. "What are you waiting for, then? Get me out of this hell hole."

Frank placed his hand over Duncan's and squeezed.

"Aye, pal. I think we've well and truly finished this shift." He smiled and held out his other hand. "Let's go, or Sadie will have my hide."

5

CHOOSE ME

There was nothing good about the situation. Megan's bridesmaid's dress was too tight, emphasizing her lumpy hips. The flowers were making her sneeze. The lilac-colored high heels pinched like a son-of-a-bitch, and her agonizing and unrequited passion for the groom was choking her.

There he stood, all 'James Bond tuxedo' and freshly shaved jaw. As his Adam's apple worked out, over and under his white collar, his startling blue eyes scanned the church, for the object of his affection, her best friend, Eva.

Megan shifted her weight, hoping to alleviate the pain in at least one foot. She stood at the back of the church, while in the small antechamber behind her, Eva leaned over and smiled indulgently as her father whispered in her ear. Some last-minute pearls of wisdom were no doubt being passed to her friend, by her picture-perfect dad. Seriously. Eva had it all.

Eva and Megan had been best friends since they had been twelve years old. Eva was the small to Megan's large, the silky to her frizz, and the shining crêpe de chine to Megan's stalwart denim. As they'd grown up, there had been nothing that they hadn't faced together, hands clasped firmly, uneven shoulders pressed close, and determination matched.

They'd made it through the inevitable obstacles life had snuck into their paths over the past twenty years, everything from Megan being brutally bullied in high school, to Eva's suspension, for allegedly cheating on her SAT's. They'd consoled each other through bad boyfriends, restrictive parental regimes, and pubescent miseries. They'd celebrated their wins together, too, including Megan landing a full-ride scholarship to Harvard while Eva was accepted at the University of North Carolina.

They'd cried dramatic buckets the day Megan left for college, but, unlike many such early formed friendships, theirs had survived all the imposed long absences from each other's lives. They had also navigated the interference of Eva's various boyfriends, jobs in other states, the loss of Megan's dad to cancer, and then the precipitous arrival of her loathsome stepfather, Hank. Always together, always tight, the two little girls—and now grown women—had stood firm in their inseparability.

When Megan's fiancé Stephen had left her, marooned and stunned in their studio apartment in Cambridge Massachusetts, it had been Eva who had driven up from North Carolina to rescue her. She'd immediately installed Megan in her minute spare bedroom, in Charlotte, much to the consternation of Megan's mother, who expected her to come home to lick her wounds. Eva had plied her with tissues, fresh strawberries, and Oreos until Megan felt able to face the world again. She had felt like Eva's beloved pet hamster during those few weeks, emerging from her bed of straw only to spin in a wheel of misery as her gentle keeper pushed sweet treats through the bars of her cage, and stroked the back of her head to ease the pain away.

She would do anything for Eva, but the day Eva had introduced her to Mike, her new firefighter boyfriend, Megan knew she was in trouble. There had been something different about this man, something unsettling. His potential to unseat her as Eva's greatest love had made Megan's throat hurt. He had stepped into the epicenter of her and Eva's friendship, inadvertently cracking it's dynamic, irreparably. It wasn't only his effect on Eva that Megan was afraid of, but also her own response to him. He was G.Q. handsome, intelligent, funny, kind and to top it all he saved lives for a living, but when, with Eva's blessing, he'd offered to escort Meghan to a swept-up work event, rather than let her turn up solo, she'd felt like Rapunzel, being rescued from the tower and, the rest was history.

Megan shook her hair from her eyes as she scanned the two sides of the small church. It was pleasantly full, just the right number of guests, equally distributed on each side of the aisle. Alternate pew ends were delicately draped with lilies and bougainvillea, and soft waves of Chopin floated down from the old pipe organ, which towered on the balcony above the gathered heads. Yes, everything was predictably perfect.

Megan felt her throat tighten. She would not cry. She would not let Eva down by making a spectacle of herself today. As Megan inhaled deeply, looking around her, Mike caught her eye, smiled, and winked. The simple action made her catch her breath. She knew that his gesture of camaraderie was genuine, but all it did was make her want to slap his perfect face. She love-hated him. She wanted to tear down the aisle and smash her lilac bouquet over his sculpted hair, seeing the spoiled petals flutter down over his gorgeous uniformed chest. She wanted to scream 'Choose *me!* Why wasn't it *me?*'

At her lack of response, Mike's expectant smile wavered. Doused in guilt, Megan swallowed hard, and with all the strength she could muster, raised her hand, nodding to him that all was well. Obvious relief flooded his face as he ran a finger around inside his collar, and rolled his shoulders back, then, leaning in toward his best man, the man of her dreams laughed softly at something his friend had said.

In an almighty twist of fate's knife, now that Megan had finally returned to Charlotte and accepted a position with a law firm that would allow her to follow her dream of defending human rights cases, Eva had announced that Mike had been offered a fire chief's position, in Nashville. After their honeymoon in Belize, they were leaving town.

A rustle behind Megan snapped her out of her reverie. Eva was ready. The ivory veil covered a flawlessly coifed up-do, and her friend's beatific smile radiated through the flimsy tulle. Her arm linked through her father's, Eva nodded to Megan, and Megan dutifully stepped behind the tiny bride and straightened out her train, smoothing the long cathedral veil over the waterfall of sparkling skirt.

Eva looked over her shoulder at Megan and mouthed, "O.K?"

Megan smiled broadly and gave her a thumbs up. "Perfect," she mouthed back.

"Love you." Eva whispered, reaching out her free hand and grabbing Megan's as she passed.

"Love you, too." Megan beamed, the image of her beloved friend losing its sharpness, as tears filled her eyes.

The opening chords of Beethoven's 9th symphony alerted the guests to Eva's imminent arrival, and, on cue, Mike turned to face the alter, pulling at his immaculate cuff. Megan focused on his capable shoulders, the ones that would never be there for *her* to cry on. She walked carefully down the aisle, toward a new future, one without the proximity of the two people she loved most in the world. With each step Megan took, Eva was getting further away from her but, as her best friend in all the world deserved, Megan found a smile, the smile she'd pull out whenever Eva needed her to, from now on. That's what best friends did for one another. That's just what they did.

6

TRIAGE

The words slipped from Grant's mouth straight onto the rug. The jagged statement flip-flopped at Sophie's feet like a goldfish, stranded and gasping for air. As his voice droned on, Sophie looked down at the slippery entity, wondering if she should perform triage, ascertain what might save it, or just leave it to end its days right there, where Grant had let it fall.

"She meant nothing to me," he repeated.

There it was again. The word-fish, slippery, agonized, deep in its death throes, and yet still alive in the room.

Grant was red in the face. *At least he had the decency to be ashamed.* Sophie watched him shift in his chair; stack and re-stack the magazines on the coffee table as he repeatedly slid his eyes up to hers and then back to the floor.

Her own voice was stuck, her vocal cords languishing in neutral. Unable to force a response, she swallowed, trying to lubricate the dry ropes stretched across the back of her throat. *Damn him.*

A shooting pain in her knee snapped Sophie's focus back to the room. The word-fish gone, leaving nothing but a tiny blank spot on the rug, she filled her lungs with acrid air. *It was too hot in here. What was he saying?*

"Soph, are you listening to me?" Grant stood and walked toward her.

He better not touch me. He better not. She stepped back, avoiding his extended hand. *I will melt. I will disintegrate if I feel his hands on me.*

"Don't." Her voice returning to her, she held her hands up in front of her chest in a warning.

"At least let me explain."

The hairs on her arms were standing to attention. *What was this sensation?* Her stomach was clenching, and her chest felt compressed, her ribs drawn inward. *Was she going to scream?* No. A laugh, harsh, bitter, and loud escaped, and then, she could not stop. The ripples forced themselves up, over and over, outward into the room, taking her with them with increasing force.

She'd read about people involuntarily laughing at funerals, but it had always seemed somewhat implausible to her, until now. Here she was, witnessing the death of her relationship—the tears running down her face caused not simply by pain but by an impulse beyond her control.

Grant was speaking. *Why couldn't she hear him?* Sophie knew that she needed to get it together, but all she could think about was gathering her possessions from the house and getting out into the fresh air.

The laughing stopped as suddenly as it had begun.

Where had she left her cashmere scarf? Was it in the bag at the bottom of the stairs? Suddenly, a succession of images flipped through her mind, the painting from above the fireplace that her grandfather had given her, the wafer-thin china tea service that her grandmother had adored, her books—so many books, the dog. *Who would get*

Frankie? Did people have custody battles over Golden Retrievers?

Grant hadn't even wanted a dog. She had been the one who'd driven past the local farm and spotted the sign. 'AKC Goldies for sale. 8 weeks.' She'd been the one who'd gone in to see the tiny, corn-colored bundles jostling, crawling over each other and yipping as she reached into the pen to pet their silken coats. Grant had stayed in the car, face buried in his phone, a disapproving grunt following her down the driveway as she'd walked toward the large barn.

When she'd come back to get him, twenty minutes later, he'd protested.

"We don't need a dog, Soph. Who'll take care of it? I'm away a lot, and you are hardly ever home. I will not walk it or pick up crap. I'm telling you now."

In response, she had laughed, cajoled and pushed him into the barn ahead of her to see the puppies.

Frankie had crawled out from under the undulating pile of golden tails, paws, and fluffy coats, and pushed his pink nose into her open palm.

"This one." She had said, looking up at Grant and smiling.

"Soph, are you listening to me? What's going on?" Startling her out of the memory, Grant spoke again, then slid his hand under her elbow and guided his now ashen wife to the sofa.

""Don't touch me." Sophie yanked her arm from his grip, her eyes flashing another warning. "Stay back".

"O.K., O.K. Jesus." Grant stepped away, raising his hands in submission. "I get it."

"Do you?" She asked, her hand wiping at her tear-stained face, her stomach sore from the pulses of laughter, and bruised from the punch of his words. "You are a walking cliché, Grant."

"Well. I guess I deserve that." He sank into the armchair and watched her lips twitch, and her face contort.

Sophie looked around her, the familiar room suddenly feeling alien and uncomfortable. *Where would she go first? To Charlotte's, of course. Where else?* Lottie had always been there for her, and the small guest room in her friend's row house across town would be her sanctuary for now.

"Can we talk about it?" Grant throttled a rolled-up magazine.

"There's nothing to talk about." She raked a hand through her long wavy hair. "I think we're done here." Sophie stood up and straightened her sweater, pulling it tidily down over the top of her jeans. "I'll come back for my things later." The words, dispassionate, after so much emotion, sounded hollow and almost comical.

"What do you mean? Are you leaving?"

""Seriously?" She swung around, anger replacing the hurt, and previous shocking mirth. Sophie walked into the kitchen, grabbed her keys, and the long leather leash hanging from the coat hook at the back door.

"Frankie, come on boy."

The dog lifted its golden head from the big circular bed in the breakfast nook. His heavy tail beat the floor, and he sniffed the air, then rose slowly and paced toward her.

"Let's go, boy."

"Are you taking Frankie?" Grant was behind her.

"Do you care?" She leant down and clipped the leash to the collar.

The back yard was damp from all the rain, the grass soft beneath her feet. She had no shoes on and wet green fingers made their way between her toes as she walked out toward the vegetable patch. She noticed that the gate, at the end of the garden, was glistening in the afternoon sun as she pushed it open and led the dog to her small car.

As she opened the trunk of the hatchback, Frankie instantly jumped in, tail wagging furiously, anticipating a walk or perhaps a run in the field.

Grant stood transfixed in the kitchen doorway. She couldn't look at him as her stomach heaved, so Sophie jumped in the driver's seat and started the car. Glancing in the rear-view mirror she wiped a hand over each eye, now red and puffy, then threw the car into reverse and edged out of the driveway.

As she drove away from the house, she saw Grant, standing, staring after her, so she pressed her bare foot down on the spongy pedal.

As soon as she was out of sight of the house, she pulled over to the shoulder and turned off the engine. She couldn't hold it in any longer. Shaking, Sophie opened the door and tumbled out and, stumbling into the long grass at the edge of the road, she bent over and vomited. All the pain, anger, shock and disappointment burned their way out of her as a stream of cars slid past. *Did they see her? Did she care?*

7

SWEET JANE

Frances sat on the steep bank of Clunie Water watching a small waterfall beat the stones at its base. Her husband, Ken, had gone into the coffee shop to get them some drinks and this being just the second day of their vacation, a deep sense of calm spread through her as she squinted into the June sun.

After completing a four-mile Highland walk, when she'd settled on the bank, she had slipped her shoes and socks off and let her bare toes sink into the cool, close-cut grass. It felt velvety under her fingertips as she leaned forward to soak in the view.

Using her hand as a visor, she scanned the steady flow of water. The narrow, sparkling ribbon was one of two rivers that sliced through the village of Braemar, a place she'd loved visiting ever since she'd been young. As they'd walked through it earlier that day, the stone cottages and eclectic collection of shops huddled close at its heart had loosed a vivid childhood memory.

When she'd been nine, her favorite uncle had brought her to Braemar after a visit to Balmoral Castle. They'd eaten ice cream from crisp cones, and then walked around the village. Eventually, they'd gone down to the river Dee to feed the clusters of ducks that gathered there, noisily demanding their dues in bread from the passersby. She'd only been back twice since then, and now, twenty-six years later, little seemed to have changed in the village. Time was frozen here.

The smell of baking was making her stomach rumble, and she hoped Ken would think to grab some snacks with their drinks. As she swiveled around to check for his familiar outline, she noticed a young girl carrying an old-fashioned baby basket along the riverbank. While she could only see the girl's profile, she looked to be in her early teens. Her long blonde hair was caught up in a half ponytail, and her dress was knee-length, floral, a soft material that clung to her legs as she moved.

Something compelled Frances to follow the girl's progress as she walked hurriedly toward the café. The young shoulders were curved into a half-moon shape as she held the baby basket close to her front. Her head dipped forward as if it were too heavy for her thin neck, and her back seemed to bow, too much for someone her age—making the entire image discomfiting. Something was off about this picture, and Frances's senses were tingling. *Was the girl in trouble, scared, running from someone, or being abused in some way?*

After a few moments, Frances shook her head at her vivid imagination, turned back toward the river and filled her lungs. Having lived in London for the past decade, the sweet novelty of clean air had yet to wear off.

As she watched, a young couple with a toddler squatted at the edge of the water and helped the little boy feed a solitary duck. Then, the image of the young girl's back, hunched over the oval basket, flashed brightly, obscuring the little family in front of her.

Once again uncomfortable, Frances blinked, and then checked her watch. *What was keeping Ken?* Standing up, she gathered her shoes and socks, and headed for the front door of the coffee shop. Several other people had settled themselves along the bank, and she smiled at the faces that turned to her as she passed, like petals toward the sun.

The stones on the path were sharp, so she dropped her shoes and slipped them on, stuffing her socks into her pocket. As she reached the door and placed her hand on the warm stone of the frame, something held her back. Rather than go inside, she sidestepped and turned toward the end of the building where the young girl had disappeared. There was a small outdoor seating area at the back of the café, and as she made her way around the building, she spied the narrow terrace with several tables scattered across it. Two were occupied and, at a third, one of the chairs had been pulled back. As she drew close, she held her breath. Under the ornate iron tabletop, pushed in close to the central leg, was the baby basket.

Frances's stomach knotted itself as she slowed her pace, tiptoeing across the remaining distance. She leaned over and peered into the basket. An infant, only weeks old, lay still. Her pristine white dress, with old-fashioned smocking across the bodice, skimmed her tiny kneecaps. The small hands were curled into fists, and translucent eyelids trembled as the child slept. A soft cotton hat matched the white shoes she wore, and a crocheted blanket was neatly folded at her feet. A bottle, still half full of milk, was wedged between the mattress and the side of the basket and, next to it, pinned to the crisp, white cotton lining, a narrow brooch in the shape of a thistle trapped a piece of paper underneath it.

Frances stared at the paper as it fluttered in the breeze, then she looked around. The two tables that had been occupied were now empty, and there was no sign of the young girl.

Turning back to the table, she reached underneath and carefully dragged the basket out to her feet. At the movement, the child lifted a fist to its eye and whimpered as Frances held her breath, willing the baby not to wake.

Frances spun around one more time, searching for the outline of that young weighted back, the blonde hair, the rounded cheek that she'd seen pass her just a few minutes ago.

As she was about to lift the basket, the back door of the coffee shop flew open, and an older man stepped out. Frances exhaled. *Perhaps this was the young girl's father, or someone else who cared about her, or this baby?*

She smiled at the man as he moved past her, his glass sweating as a trickle of froth slopped over its edge. Her stomach dipped with disappointment as he passed by and sat at a table behind her, without so much as a glance at the bundle at her feet.

She looked down at the baby. The grey-blue eyes were open now, assessing her, so she knelt on the ground and reached into the basket, her finger crooked as if ready for a bird's wiry foot. The child wrapped its miniature fingers around hers and pursed its lips, making a sucking sound that caused Frances to swallow.

The memory of sweet Jane, their beloved daughter, who had passed away the year before, from S.I.D.S., brought Frances's eyes tightly shut as her heart took flight in her chest. She couldn't let that pain back in. She simply couldn't.

After a few moments, as her thumping heart began to settle, she looked over at the café, gently eased her finger out of the child's grasp and stood up. She glanced back at the elderly man who was now reading a newspaper.

"Excuse me." She moved close to his table.

He lowered his paper and smiled. "Yes?"

"Did you see the baby's mother inside?" She jabbed a thumb over her shoulder.

He frowned. "Baby?"

"Over there." She pointed.

"Oh, right." He paused. "I don't know. The place is quite busy, though." He shrugged. "She could be in there."

Frances thanked him and returned to the basket. The little girl was gumming her fist, her eyes flitting between the overhead clouds and the edges of her basket cocoon. Frances leaned down, gathered up the woven handles, and lifted the basket to her front. It was surprisingly heavy.

"Come on, little one. Let's see if we can find your mummy." She whispered.

The child began to cry, her lower lip curling back as a tiny tongue rippled inside the rosy cave of her mouth. Frances shushed her and read the words on the fluttering paper as she headed for the Inn.

My darling daughter,

I'm very sorry. You were so loved, but I was afraid. I will always miss you.

Mummy.

Her throat narrowing, she turned to see Ken walking toward her, two covered cups and a crinkled paper bag held close to his middle. "What've you got there?" He nodded at the basket.

"You're not going to believe this." She moved the basket toward him, watching as he leaned over and squinted at the baby. "Someone left the poor wee mite out here." She gestured toward the table behind her. "It was a young girl. I saw her pass me, down by the river, and then she came around the back here and just left the basket under a table."

Her husband shook his head. "Really?" He spun around, a frown creasing his brow. "Surely not."

The child whimpered, so Frances gently set the basket down and kneeled next to it on the moist grass. "What should we do?" She let the child grab her index finger again, then looked up at her husband, who was scanning the surrounding tables.

"We should take her inside. Ask if her mother's in there." He eyed her, and when she stayed silent, he continued. "Frances?"

She felt a sudden rush of adrenaline, a wash of heat creeping up her chest and across her throat. "She's been abandoned?" She avoided Ken's questioning eyes. "Read the note." She pointed at the paper pinned to the lining of the basket.

"Frances, darling. We have to take her inside and find out where her mother is." The gentle tone of his voice released the tears that had been lurking behind her eyes. "Fran?"

As a single tear trickled down her cheek, she forced a swallow, gently releasing the grip of the tiny fist from around her finger. "I know," she gulped. "I know."

He set the cups, and paper bag, on the tabletop next to him, leaned down and lifted the basket. "Come on, love. Let's go inside." He gestured toward the café. "We'll sort it out."

Frances stood up, her chest weighted, and her limbs numb. "Ken?" She watched as he shifted the basket higher up in front of his middle.

"Yes, love?" His kind eyes held hers.

"She has the same color eyes as Jane. She's about the

same age as when…" The last word caught in her throat as he took the handles of the basket in one hand and held his other out to her.

"It's not Jane, darling." His voice was rough. "This wee one needs her mum."

With a strange ticking at her temple, and feeling as if her insides might explode, Frances nodded. "I know that." She caught her breath. "But she was just left out here, all alone." She tugged at his hand. "Who would know?" She glanced around herself, seeing the empty tables and chairs scattered across the patio—blind witnesses to the desperate and uncharacteristic act that she was contemplating.

Ken took an audible breath and dipped his chin toward the baby. "We would know, sweetheart. We would."

8

THE TERMITE TENT

The stained tent stretched over the house, her canvas tentacles driven into the ground by cruel metal pins. Each long pin, caked with the mud and sand of previous stakeouts, held her tightly in place. Underneath her skin, the chemicals did their work on the wood-eating termites, whose tiny jaws working on the bones of the house were destroying it from the inside out, like bacteria.

It was a cold day, and the humans were gone, for now. A sharp wind wriggled its way under one of the tent's edges, and she shivered. The chilly breath slid up under her belly, toward the roof of the house.

She could still feel the vibration of the munching. It tickled where her sides touched the timber-framed walls. Would the wood-eaters ever be full, or would the chemicals sprayed on the wood turn them into tiny curling balls, before the house fell to the ground, in a pile of sticks and broken glass? The tent sighed with the winds and reached her fingers deeper into the dirt. She was here to ensure the wood-eaters died and, cold or not, she would do her job.

The sky stretched grey and dull overhead, and even the

birds had left her alone today. Oddly, she missed their sharp claws, and pecking beaks, as she scanned her surroundings for company. Raindrops began to patter on her top, and as dark clouds closed in, she felt tiny rivulets of water running down her folds and begin to puddle around the determined pins.

Eventually, a small human appeared in the street in front of her, riding a bicycle, then a larger human trotted close behind, calling out instructions.

"Keep going. We're almost there. Good boy."

The tent wondered where these humans lived. Did their home have wood-eaters in its bones too? She liked wrapping the houses where small humans lived. Those houses felt warmer somehow, even once they were coated with chemicals and empty of life.

The rain picked up momentum, and she felt the weight of accumulated water on her back. Who had decided that this would be her life? Who at the tent-birthing den had picked her for this purpose? There were many other jobs she could have done, like cover a truck, heavy with smooth rocks from the river, or protect a group of humans sleeping on a mountainside. She could have shrouded a sleek boat in the harbor or even a fragrant woodpile in a peaceful back yard. She could have been so many things but, here she was, trapping chemical-coated wood-eaters and being pecked by ignorant birds, trying to get at the tiny toxic carcasses under her skin.

She could even have been something whimsical, like a circus tent. Yes, a big top. It was her dream to be clean and colorful, with a fancy fringe, or perhaps a double-layered top. She'd stretch high over hundreds of happy humans, the small ones smiling at the lions, elephants, and clowns parading underneath her shelter. With her ribs and diaphragm, formed by long ropes crisscrossing the air above their heads, she'd have made a great big top.

The wind died down, and then the rain stopped. Funny how those two elements always followed each other so closely. They were fated to exist together, just like her and the wood-eaters.

9

SERENDIPITY

The letter slid under the door with an almost inaudible swish. Vaguely aware of it, Harry lifted his head from the pillow and momentarily forgot where he was. Frowning, he sat up, swung his legs over the edge of the bed, and stared at the window that was shrouded in heavy black-out drapes.

He stretched, lifted his watch from the bedside table, then reached out and pulled back the edge of one curtain. As a sliver of light fell across the luminous dial in his palm, he could see it was 6.43 a.m., and, as he looked around, his foggy mind cleared itself as the hotel room materialized. He was in Vienna and, if he was not mistaken, this was Sunday.

The trip had gone well, and his client had signed the contract for the design of a new wing to the Symphonic library, a landmark project his architectural firm had been chasing for over a year. Harry had been in Vienna for three days now and was scheduled to travel home to London the following morning. He had deliberately allowed himself an extra day, after his meetings, to enjoy some downtime, specifically to visit the national library in the Hofburg Palace. He loved the serenity within the 18th Century Baroque walls, the smell of the floor-to-ceiling, leather-bound maps, and treasured manuscripts, the lustrous wood paneling. He especially liked to tip his head back and soak in Daniel Gran's luminous fresco, that covered the domed ceiling.

A strip of white catching his eye, Harry got up and moved slowly toward the crack of light seeping under the door. The letter lay stark against the dark brown carpet, and as he eyed it, he scrubbed his palm over his short-cropped hair.

He leaned down and picked up the envelope, noticing the heavy quality of the paper stock, textured like papyrus under his fingers, and his curiosity peaked as he flipped on the light, illuminating the room behind him.

Walking back to the bed, he sat on the end and ripped open the unmarked envelope. Inside was a simple sheet of paper, of equally good quality, folded in three even sections.

Dear Martin, I know this will come as a shock, but I couldn't help myself but write after I saw you in the lobby yesterday. I couldn't believe it was you, after all these years. I'm staying here until Tuesday and would love to meet you for a drink, just to catch up. Please call me in room 563, and we'll arrange a convenient time. With love, Olivia.

Harry turned the paper over, searching for some further explanation, or clue to the sender's identity. He didn't know anyone called Olivia, and who was this Martin person? As he let the page drop to his thigh, he guessed that someone on the hotel staff was going to be in deep trouble when he turned this letter in to the reception desk.

Throwing the letter onto the bed, he stood and opened the

curtains, letting the bright April light flood the room. Vienna lay below his window, the breath of musicians, the smell of roasting coffee, the thrum of the streets of this city of music awaited him. With nothing on his agenda but time to do whatever he wished, he didn't want to waste any more of it inside this room.

Having showered and dressed, rather than use the elevator, Harry walked down the stairs then paced across the spacious lobby. Feeling his leather-soled shoes slipping on the polished marble floor, he negotiated his way around an older couple dragging two enormous suitcases, then he carefully walked up to the concierge desk in the corner, by the main entrance.

"Good morning. This was put under my door by mistake." He placed the envelope down on the leather blotter.

"Apologies, Mr. Bannister. We were asked to deliver it to you this morning." The young man adjusted his tight collar, the color rising slightly in his cheeks.

"Yes, but I'm not this Martin person," he pointed at the letter. "It's not for me." He looked inquiringly at the concierge.

"The lady was most insistent, sir. She wrote the envelope right here at the desk and told me specifically that it was for you. She said she knew you, from many years ago, and had seen you in the lobby yesterday evening."

The young man looked both apologetic and uncomfortable, and seeing it, Harry felt suddenly sorry for him.

"Is this lady still here?" he asked, looking around.

"I believe she is having breakfast, sir." The young man pointed toward the heavy, French paneled doors at the far side of the lobby.

"Fine. Then I'll go and tell her myself that she's mistaken. What does she look like?"

"She has long dark hair, a small lady, wearing a yellow jacket." The concierge nodded deferentially as Harry picked up the letter and spun around on his slippery shoes.

The bright dining room was busy, with most of the tables occupied, and the rich smell of freshly baked pastries and fragrant coffee that met him instantly reminded Harry how hungry he was. Focusing on his mission, he assessed the many occupants, looking for a yellow jacket, his eyes finally settling on a table in the corner.

The woman was facing away from him, looking out over the gardens. Her back was long and narrow, lustrous dark hair tumbling down between her shoulder blades, in sharp contrast to her sunflower-colored jacket. The window she stared at was slightly open, and the white net curtains billowed inward, shards of sunlight softly dappling them.

Pressing his shoulders down, Harry approached the table, suddenly less confident in his objective. There was something familiar in the way she held herself that gave him pause. *Perhaps he did know her?*

Standing behind her chair, he cleared his throat, just as the woman turned her head and jumped as she caught sight of him.

"I'm sorry. I didn't mean to startle you," he said, walking to her side so she could see him more clearly.

"Oh, it's O.K. I just got a fright," she said, smiling up at him, her palm pressed to her chest.

Harry caught his breath. That face. *Did he know that face?* Her hair was raven-dark and swept to one side, across a broad brow. Her eyes were startling, one a deep blue and the other green, and as she smiled, a tiny dimple appeared on either side of her mouth, the sight of which robbed him of speech.

When the silence between them became cumbersome,

Harry gathered himself and spoke. "I received this letter by mistake." He held the envelope out to her. "I'm not Martin."
Would she ask him to sit?

The woman looked down at his hand and slowly, comprehension clouded her face. "Oh." She sighed.

"It's not for me," he said, instantly angry at himself for restating the obvious. *What was wrong with him?*

She gently took the letter from him. "I'm sorry about that." She took a deep breath and straightened her spine. "I thought you were someone else." She tucked the letter into her purse and then finally raised her eyes back to Harry's.

Another interminable silence ensued, an eternity of painful nothingness. Then, she smiled that smile again. "By way of apology, would you like to join me for coffee?" She indicated the chair opposite her, and Harry exhaled.

"Actually, I would," he said, smiling, suddenly immensely grateful for the serendipitous misunderstanding that had brought him to this table, this moment, and all the possibilities it promised.

10

SNOW

R achel lay on her side, and the snow had drifted in against the concave bay of her stomach. It gathered in a white slope, ascending gently from the ground up to the top of her rib cage.

There was no single word to describe how cold she was. If there was a German word, she'd forgotten it, and even her native Polish escaped her now. *What did it matter anyway?* Whatever language she had forgotten made no difference to the fact that she was probably going to die here.

She felt the wind lift the flap of her coat, and fill her skirt, her thin stockings and hole-riddled socks no match for the insistent breeze. She wasn't far from the road but, after two days of walking, with little to no rest, and nothing but an apple, a hard-boiled egg, and a small flask of water to sustain her, she knew she had probably strayed from the track.

It had been difficult to stay focused, with the billowing snow, and wind, biting painfully into her face, hands, and shins. Her progress had been slow, her boots sinking until the cold whiteness slid inside them, numbing her feet, as she hoisted each one up and placed it down in front of the other, like matching anvils.

Next to her head the coarse grasses were long but bent over, almost flat to the ground under the weight of the snow. In the corner of her eye, she saw a clump of wheat stalks woven into a complex, frosty white cage that arched up from the ground below.

Her eyelashes were heavy with crystals that melted painfully back into her eyes as she blinked.

There was no smell that she could discern. The winter, and the war, had killed the fragrant meadows and crops that she'd loved to walk among as a child. Now, all she saw when she looked around her was a white wasteland.

If she closed her eyes and breathed in the cold, embracing it, offering it a home in her lungs, then perhaps it would spirit her away from here. Perhaps it would take her to Yanesh, wherever he was.

It had been four months since they'd seen each other. When they'd escaped from the camp, he'd left her at his sister Serena's farm, near Krakow, before leaving with the resistance. Serena had been good to Rachel, giving her sanctuary from the hell she'd lived through, coaxing her back to health, until a week ago, when the Russians had burst through the door and taken Serena away.

Rachel had been in the outhouse and, to her gut-twisting shame, she had stayed there, trembling and crying into her fist as the truck bumped away into the distance with her one and only friend in the back.

She'd stayed in the little wooden hut until the sun went down that day, then she'd crept into the house to gather her things. Too afraid to sleep inside, she'd spent the next few nights in the woodshed until finally she'd known it was time to move on.

With a few morsels of food in a sack, and wearing the warmest clothes she owned, she'd walked away from the one place she'd finally begun to feel safe again.

At the memory of Serena, Rachel felt a river of pain wash over her. *How could she have been so cowardly?* Serena had hidden her for months, and all Rachel could do was squat in the dirty outhouse, watching as her savior was dragged away at gunpoint. Rachel's shame was as cold and unyielding as the ground underneath her.

Another icy breath made her cough, sending her empty stomach into a spasm. *Just let me go.*

As she lay motionless, the cheek that was pressed into the ground felt a tremor, as if the earth was moving beneath her jaw. She stilled her breathing, scared to move in case the tremor came again, and she missed it. Then, the frozen ground began to tremble, and as Rachel held her breath, she heard the familiar grind of a gearbox. At the jarring sound, she lifted her head, her woolen scarf heavy with moisture, and looked back in the direction she'd come.

A few hundred yards away, a large vehicle rumbled toward her. Within seconds, several scenarios passed through her mind. *It was the Russians, back to get her, poor Serena having given her location away when they tortured her. It was the Germans, tracking down runaways, and returning them to the camps. It was Yanesh, having been to the farm and found her gone; he'd scoured the surrounding villages looking for her.*

Her heart picked up a beat, and she heard the air hissing from the vehicle's brakes as it stopped. She knew she could not get up, regardless of whoever was behind that wheel. No, this would be the defining moment of her life.

As she lay still, waiting for the strike of a Russian rifle, or the shove of a German boot, she heard a voice. It was soft and female. Opening one crusted eyelid, she saw a shock of red hair, a white cape and cap, and a pair of blue eyes. Then, she felt the press of fingers on her neck, gentle but firm.

"She's alive." The woman called back to the vehicle, in Polish.

Rachel lifted her head as the nurse slipped an arm under her shoulder and then slowly helped her to sit up. She could see that the bus was grey and battered, with a large red cross on the front, above its cracked windshield.

"Come with me, my sweet." The voice was like honey.

Rachel felt herself being lifted to her feet and led by the elbow to the bus. The door stood ajar, and the driver smiled down at her as the nurse helped her lift one stiff leg, then the other, up onto the step.

"So glad we found you." The driver's voice was rough, but the kindness of his words brought her to tears.

Rachel pursed her blue lips, trying to form a word.

"Tha... thank."

Understanding, the driver nodded and waved toward the back of the bus, as the nurse helped her move into a seat.

With a thin blanket tucked around her legs, Rachel wiped a small spy hole in the condensation on the window. The surrounding countryside was a blur, and she could see nothing ahead except the swirl of new snow. She leaned her spent shoulder against the window and closed her eyes, and as the bus wheezed, and lurched forward, she swallowed against the knot of relief forming in her throat. If she could stay alive, she might see this place again. She might see the fields, rich with wheat, rye, and barley. She might see Yanesh, and hopefully, dear Serena, once more. *If she could just stay alive.*

11

THE BOOK

The car was just what Grace had wanted—gently used and inexpensive. After eight years in the Marines, she could pilot a Viper helicopter like the best of them but ask her to pick a decent used car, and she was stuck. Her brother, Andrew, had found this one in the newspaper, being sold by a man in town. He had checked it over for her, so she was happy that it was a good buy. Thirty to her twenty-eight, Andrew still took care of her when she let him.

Grace shivered, and turned up the heater, slid the seat a little further forward and adjusted the rear-view mirror. It felt good to be behind the wheel again.

With both Grace and Andrew deployed to Afghanistan, they knew that their mother had gone prematurely grey, sleeping only intermittently for the duration of their absences, dreading the phone call in the middle of the night, with news she could not bear to hear. But they were both home to stay now, and compared to so many, they'd been lucky.

Grace pressed her foot on the gas and the little Ford jumped forward. She'd have to learn the personality of the car, the precise balance of clutch and accelerator, but it always took a while, with a new vehicle.

"We'll get to know each other, girl," she said, patting the dashboard.

The town of Concord, Massachusetts, was quiet this Sunday morning. Her mother was making lunch and had invited both her and Andrew over. Grace had arrived back from Kabul first, and three weeks later, Andrew had landed at Boston Logan. She and her mother had driven down to meet him and, before splintering off to their own apartments, they'd both spent the first few days in their old rooms at their mother's house, adjusting to their surroundings, and reacquainting themselves with being part of the family unit again.

Concord was where they'd grown up and Grace was proud of her little town, and the marks it had left on history, with the legacies of its eminent literary citizens, Emerson, Hawthorn, Alcott and Thoreau. As everyone here learned in the local school, as taught by her own mother, the town had also been the seat of transcendentalism, and crucial in the establishment of the underground railway.

Despite its literary and social pedigree, there wasn't much to do around here now, but after the brutal mountain landscape of Afghanistan, it was paradise to be home, especially in time for Christmas.

Grace drove down Main Street noting the familiar pharmacy, café, the general store and the town's one crosswalk. As she moved on, the sight of the old street lanterns wrapped with festive lights and fresh green garlands, made her smile.

She turned the corner into her mother's street and, with the change in direction, heard a loud clunk from the back of the car. Grace's heart sank as she imagined the worst. *Had they been duped by the sweet old guy who'd sold it to them? Had some vital engine component just fallen into the street?*

She looked in the rear-view mirror, scanning the road behind her, but could see nothing.

As she turned into her mother's driveway, the back of the car swung around and she heard the sound again, but this time it seemed to come from the trunk.

She climbed out of the car, walked around back and opened the trunk. Inside, she spotted a dark brown rag, rough in texture and bound with a thin leather strap. Leaning in, she picked up the bundle, instantly realizing that the rag was wrapped around something hard.

Grace carefully unbuckled the strap and removed the cloth, seeing that it had covered an old, leather-bound book. The cover was in pretty good condition and as she turned it over in her hands, she could see that its wafer-thin internal pages were edged with gold leaf. The cover was dark red and there had been gold lettering on the front which was now illegible.

She slowly opened the front cover, hoping to find something to identify the book's age and ownership. On the delicate, yellowing flyleaf was an inscription, the handwriting formal and loopy, the ink pale-blue and faded by time.

My dearest nephew, this is a book of little women. I entreat you to be patient with its contents and its author. It was written with the affection of family in mind and you are my family, my dearest. Fondly, Aunt Louisa.

For a moment Grace was still, the open book heavy in her hands. *It couldn't be possible, could it? Could this be the Louisa?* Turning to the next page, Grace's eyes widened as she saw the title, in flowery script, 'Little Women', by Louisa

May Alcott. She turned another page, and the opening line she knew so well, from the many times her mother had read it to her as a child, jumped out at her.

"Christmas won't be Christmas without any presents," grumbled Jo, lying on the rug.

Grace's heart leapt as she looked at the familiar words. She ran a finger over the text, hoping to feel with her fingertips the truth of what she was seeing. She'd loved this book growing up, and the idea that it had taken place here, in Concord, written by a local heroine, had always thrilled her. Louisa May Alcott had been considered a trail blazer in her time, and Grace liked to think that she too, as a female helicopter pilot, was doing her bit to fly Concord's flag and perpetuate the momentum created by the petite lady, who's work she now held in her hands.

No sooner had her heart leapt with excitement than she was struck by the reality that this treasure in fact belonged to the old man she'd bought the car from. She knew without question that she'd have to return it to him.

Placing the book on the passenger seat, she started the car and reversed back out into the street. Lunch with her family forgotten, Grace drove back to the house on Canal Street, where they had picked up the car a couple of days before.

The small house was still. Grace rang the doorbell and waited on the quaint porch, rubbing her hands together against the cold and watching small tendrils of breath smoke from her mouth.

"Who is it?" A gravelly voice came from behind the door.

"Hello, sir. It's Grace Fielding. I bought your Ford the

other day." She leaned in, noticing the varnish on the door frame, peeling and curled up like many sets of dusty wings.

After a few moments the man spoke, the door remaining closed. "It was sold as seen. You can't give it back now."

"It's not that. I found a book in the trunk. I wanted to return it." Getting no response, Grace spoke again. "Are you there?"

"You keep it. It was probably my wife's, and she passed on two years ago. I don't read much, so…"

"But sir, I think it's valuable. It looks like an Alcott, I mean, possibly an original copy. And it's signed."

The door opened slightly, and the man pushed his wizened face into the small gap he'd created. "You keep it, my dear. She'd have wanted it to go to someone who'd appreciate it."

Grace felt her face flush. She was growing uncomfortable and needed him to understand that this book was worth something, was possibly a piece of history that might even belong in the museum in town.

"But sir, I really….."

The door closed slowly but firmly, and Grace stood still for a few minutes, the book held close to her chest.

From behind the door she heard his voice again. "Keep it and enjoy it in good health, my dear. By rights the book belongs to you now." He chuckled. "Besides, Christmas won't be Christmas, without presents."

D an had found out that he had cancer two months
ago, while sitting in the office waiting for the
doctor to come in. His medical file had been lying
on the desk and as he read his name, upside down on the
dingy cover, his curiosity had prickled. As a blast of dry heat
sank down from the vent above his head, the corner of a
white page, protruding slightly from inside the file, had fluttered—beckoning him closer. He'd battled with the dueling
forces that whispered, each in a respective ear, *leave it alone,*
pick it up, leave it alone.

Straying from the straight and narrow path he generally
liked to inhabit, Dan had leaned across the desk and picked
up the file. He'd figured that the contents were about him,
therefore belonged to him.

Opening the folder had only felt a little wrong, and he'd
flipped through the contents, scanning for anything that
looked ominous or remotely decipherable from the pages of
medical terminology lying limp within his fingers. Feeling
discouraged by the jargon and sensing a large slice of truth in

the adage that those who eavesdrop seldom hear anything good about themselves, he'd begun to tidy the papers back into the folder. Suddenly the word *carcinoma* had swum into his vision and dragged the breath out of him. Dan's stomach had tied itself into a knot as he'd frantically looked again, trying to re-locate the foul word, hoping he had misread something in haste.

After a few moments, the doctor's voice permeated the heavy wooden door, as he spoke to someone outside in the hallway. Dan had hurriedly stacked the papers, slid them inside the folder, and sat back in his chair, his heart racing at his duplicitousness. He'd been terrified at what he was about to hear, and yet still acknowledged a modicum of guilt at his snooping. He'd silently counseled himself, accepting the ludicrous nature of that guilt—after all, this was *his* body and *his* medical information—then, the doctor had come into the room.

"Daniel. Sorry to keep you waiting." Dr. Easman had slid behind the desk and settled into his wing-backed chair. Gathering Dan's file onto his lap, he'd begun flipping through the pages.

"So, we got the test results back." He'd raised his eyes to his patient's.

Dan had nodded silently, afraid his voice would betray him if he tried to use it.

"It's not good news, I'm afraid." The doctor had nodded to himself, requiring nothing from Dan, as he dropped his gaze again and scrutinized one of the papers.

Dan had stayed still, afraid that if he moved, he would disintegrate into a slick puddle of matter, nothing left but a small glistening pool of his former self on the floor.

"There were malignant cells in the biopsy. It appears we

are looking at an advanced stage of melanoma." Easman had placed the folder carefully on his desk and looked Dan in the eye.

The biopsy of the cyst under his arm had been done two weeks earlier, and Dan regretted not having told his wife, Clare, anything about it. He'd suddenly wanted her there, more than anything in the world, and as he'd struggled to hear Dr. Easman speak, he'd allowed fear to block his ears.

Clare would have been taking notes, in one of those spiral-bound books she liked. She would have been asking questions, nodding her understanding and pressing her cool fingers onto his arm to reassure him that they were going to be fine.

"Daniel, is your wife aware of what's going on?" The doctor tapped into his thoughts, cornering him.

"No. I didn't want to worry her, until we knew what it was." Dan's voice cracked as he spoke, and he cleared his throat, embarrassed.

"Well, I think it would be best if you brought her up to speed." Dr. Easman's professional veneer had warped a little, as Dan recognized pity in the man's face.

Dan had nodded, gathered his numb legs underneath him, and made to get up.

Extending a hand toward him, palm down, Easman had continued.

"We need to talk about a treatment plan. It should be soon and, as I'm sure you've probably surmised, we need to attack this full force. Can you and your wife come in on Friday? I'll have Sally set up an hour consult so we can talk everything through."

Dan had lowered himself back into the chair. Accepting that he had obviously not been dismissed yet, he'd tried to focus on Easman's face as the lips continued to move. He'd heard the words *stage three*, *metastasized,* then he'd heard nothing more.

His mind had been racing. The thought that his body had let him down, this badly, was overwhelming all other points of focus. It was, after all, the ultimate betrayal—to have your own physiology become the enemy. He was only sixty-four years old, and just the previous week had accepted early retirement from the bank he'd managed for the past seventeen years. He and Clare had spent the weekend looking at travel brochures and planning the trip of a lifetime—excited to finally have the time, and the means, to visit some of the places they had always dreamed of seeing. The humbling architecture of the Duomo in Florence, the towering walls of the coliseum in Rome; the breath-taking Sagrada Familia cathedral in Barcelona, the blue mosque in Istanbul, the acropolis in Athens and, the pièce de résistance, the amphitheatre at Epidavros in the Peloponnese.

"Daniel?" Dr. Easman had said his name again, snapping him out of his reverie.

"Yes, I'll talk to Clare." He'd had felt a sudden, irrational irritation with Easman's calm tone. How many times had he delivered this soliloquy, Dan wondered? How many people had this doctor torn the breath from as he sat in that red-leather chair, with its studded back and padded wings? Dan had wondered how many of the congregation of sick people that once occupied the waiting room, and circulated in and out of this office, had fallen apart at the word *malignant*. How many had cried angry tears, yelled in frustration, or perhaps laughed at the bad joke they were hearing, and how many were, like him, shocked into silence—the ability to react or absorb the information they had just received evading them.

"We were planning a vacation." Dan had blurted the words, rising once again from the chair. "Eight weeks in Europe." He'd looked at the doctor blankly and shrugged.

"Well, we can talk about that on Friday. I'd advise against leaving right now, as I said, we need to start treatment as soon as we can."

Dr. Easman had risen, extending a hand to Dan, indicating that he could now leave.

"So, we're talking chemo, radiation?" Dan's irritation had bubbled up again and he'd ignored the hand on offer.

"Yes, that'd be my advice. Surgery, then a combination of both chemotherapy and radiation." Easman had studied Dan's mouth.

"I'll talk to Clare." He'd repeated himself, the only statement that came to mind.

"O.K., good. I'm sorry it's not better news." The tone of the doctor's voice had been even, and once again genuinely filled with concern, and Dan had turned and pulled on his coat.

"You and me both."

Dan remembered floating in a bubble of suspended belief as he walked out of the waiting area and into reception. As he'd left the building, a thin veil of rain had covered his face as he'd stepped out onto the sidewalk. His mind had gone back to their trip, to seeing Rome, Istanbul, and Greece, and despite all the thoughts tumbling around inside the empty drum of his head, there were three things he knew for sure. He wasn't ready to die. They were going on that trip, and he wasn't going to tell Clare about his illness. At least not yet.

～

Clare knew that more than any of the other places he'd earmarked, Dan had always wanted to visit Epidavros, to see with his own eyes the magnificent amphitheater, nestled between the mountains and the green of the surrounding Argolis region of Greece.

When he had accepted early retirement from the bank, they had decided that this was the one truly extravagant thing they would do. They'd take their dream European trip culminating in Greece, to explore the Peloponnese, visit a couple of the idyllic islands, and then see Epidavros—a place he had read about, and pored over pictures of, for as long as she could remember.

He had been silent for much of the journey from Athens, and with her nose pressed close to the window, Clare watched the scenery gradually change—the city landscape falling away to leave dusty brown plains, with a few sturdy shrubs grappling for survival on intermittent mounds of parched earth. She had thought it would be greener, and, when she asked about it a few moments earlier, the tour guide said it would be, when they got higher into the mountains.

Clare sat back and fought her slight disappointment at what she was seeing, and as the bus jolted on, and Dan silently read his guidebook next to her, she felt sleep pulling at her.

The vehicle's momentum faltered slightly as the driver braked. Clare, nudged from her slumber, noticed a small figure, hunched at the waist, walking in the road ahead. Dressed in black from head to toe, the woman drove a scrawny goat before her, with taps from a thin stick. As the bus swung out gently into the road and passed the petite woman, Clare turned in her seat to get a better view.

The small face was impossibly wrinkled, sun browned, and surrounded by a black scarf, tucked tightly in place under the chin, giving a nun-like appearance. As Clare watched, the woman tapped the rear end of the goat again and seemed to ignore the presence of the bus altogether, intent only on her mission.

On a reflex, Clare reached for the camera, but it was snugly encased inside the expensive bag Dan had insisted they buy for the trip. There was no time to grab it in order to capture this image so, seeing him, nose still deep in his book, she sat back and sighed.

The bus moved on, and Clare returned her attention to the road ahead.

The journey from Athens had taken two-and-a-half hours, so far, and the group was growing restless when finally, the tour guide's voice crackled over the P.A. system, announcing that they were approaching Epidavros. The welcome spiel rolled off his tongue as the other passengers began to gather their bags and cameras.

They parked in an open lot, amidst a much greener and more imposing environment than the surrounding country-side. Beside her, Dan shoved his guidebook into his backpack as the tour guide explained that this was the birthplace of Asclepius, the son of Apollo—and that the Sanctuary at Epidavros had been known as the most celebrated healing center in the classical world.

Around them, the group shimmied out of their respective seats and moved toward the front of the bus. She and Dan, as was their habit, sat tight and waited for everyone else to disembark, and as the human trail petered out, Dan rose and put out his hand to her, helping her up. She smiled at him, and he reciprocated, squeezing her fingers, indicating his excite-ment at being here—finally—in a place he'd studied and dreamed of visiting for years.

Dan was obviously awe-struck, and, as soon as his bus-weary feet hit the dusty ground, he wandered absently away from Clare, as if she had never been with him at all. As the magnificence of the amphitheater rose ahead of them, he seemed to be transported. The genius of this example, of 3rd Century engineering, and craftsmanship had encapsulated both his heart and attention, and she smiled indulgently at her husband's rapture.

Clare carried the camera case, and the packed lunch the hotel had provided for them, and followed in Dan's wake, leaving enough distance for him to feel solitary—without truly being alone. She sensed his need to experience this in isolation, to absorb this wonder in silence, and she respected that.

As she watched his back moving slowly away from her, she noticed a new curve to his shoulders, and that his gait was somewhat heavier than usual. He was tired, she knew that, and he needed this break, as she did herself, but something else had been tugging at the back of her mind, a sense that there was more to his new, brooding silences. Dan had never been a secret-keeper, but Clare knew enough to know that something was bothering him that he hadn't shared with her, and she missed her mischievous, fun loving husband.

Walking into the amphitheater was indeed awe inspiring. True to the tradition of the Greek engineers of the era, it was lovingly embraced by the surrounding mountains, and the green of the natural landscape. The groves and shrubs, all but undisturbed by the towering stone structure, served as the backdrop to the magnificent stage. As the rows of marble benches rose in perfect curves, up and up, toward the great height at the back, Clare caught her breath. The design was incredibly emotive, like a semi-circle of arms, serene and imposing, waiting to embrace their audience.

Thankfully there weren't too many people on their tour.

She had counted eleven, including herself and Dan, so as the small group filtered in and around the amphitheater, their presence caused but a few ripples of movement in the scene of ancient perfection before her.

Dan was walking around one of the lower rows of benches, stopping to run his hand over the marble, then looking down, rubbing the fine particles of history between finger and thumb. Clare thought she saw him shake his head, though it was almost imperceptible, then after a few minutes, she saw his head snap up.

Suddenly aware that he had abandoned her, he turned and scanned the auditorium. She raised a hand and waved, making herself visible. Dan spotted her and waved back then shrugged his shoulders, his hands held out in front of him, begging her pardon, as he smiled sheepishly. She smiled back and patted the air, letting him know he should go ahead.

While she had his attention, Clare pointed to the top of the auditorium, indicating that she would head up there. Dan nodded his understanding and then, to her surprise, lifted a hand to his mouth and blew her a single kiss. She smiled and caught it with her free hand, then pressed her fist to her chest, a simple exchange, but one they'd been making with the other since before they were married, thirty-four years ago.

With his kiss warming her palm, she turned and started to climb. After only a few minutes, Clare's legs began to tremble with the unaccustomed exertion. As small beads of sweat bubbled onto her forehead and upper lip, she looked up at the clear blue sky, for once wishing for some sympathetic clouds to shield her from the April sun's harsh rays. Wiping at her face with the arm of her T-shirt, she continued to climb. One hundred and thirteen steps the guidebook said and, Clare counted them off as she went.

Reaching the top row of the 15,000-seat amphitheater, she

turned and looked down. Dan stood in the center of the stage looking up toward the benches. She waved to catch his attention again and then, just as the guidebooks said she would, she heard his voice, no more than a whisper.

"I love you. Thanks for this." He hesitated. "Clare, I need to tell you something."

13

MÉLANGE

T he front of the restaurant had seen better days. The dark green canopy was faded, and weather-worn, and the small carriage lights on either side of the front door looked like brass, under all the tarnish.

I suppose I could write that up as a patina, Amy thought.

The small, leaded windows glimmered with a warm orange light from within and, along with the peeling painted windowsills, gave a Dickensian feel to the frontage. Feeling optimistic, Amy grabbed her camera and snapped a couple of pictures to add to the article.

Her table was booked for 7.00 pm, so, with a few minutes to spare, she'd walked around the neighborhood to get a sense of the environment. Amy always found that when critiquing a restaurant, her readers enjoyed hearing about the location and surroundings almost as much as the food.

She loved reviewing Scottish restaurants and had jumped at this assignment to travel to the picturesque village of Crail, on the Fife Coast. Despite having moved away many years ago, the sense of coming home had never waned whenever she came back to review places in her homeland.

The small, unassuming Scottish towns with their narrow streets, and history oozing from every pore, never failed to delight her. While some of the establishments she'd reviewed in the past had left her craving a simple slice of toast, just to cleanse her palate, others had left her floating on a tide of such delectably fragrant and fresh cuisine, that she couldn't write fast enough to capture her enthusiasm. In some cases, she'd even scribbled notes on napkins (cloth or otherwise) between courses, apologizing for her vandalism to the raised eyebrows of the management.

As far as eateries, Scotland had so many hidden gems, and she felt, that over the years, her reviews had shed light on a few of these under-valued national treasures. Amy was hopeful that Mélange would prove to be another of them. However, a recent experience with a Glaswegian restaurateur, called Hamish, had shaken her faith in Scottish cuisine a little. Despite Amy voicing her concerns, Hamish had staunchly stood behind his concept of deep-fried Mars Bar served with crème frâiche, and a beer reduction. Nevertheless, she'd remained optimistic that her motherland could redeem itself this evening.

Picking up the menu, she scanned the name Mélange. It was in an old-fashioned script at the top of a single sheet of butter-colored parchment paper. So far so good. It was crisp and clean, with no tackiness under her fingers, which was always an instant red flag as to what to expect from the kitchen.

As her eyes traveled down the list of first courses, Amy found herself sincerely hoping that the chef, in his choice of dishes, had focused on the *mixture* interpretation of the word Mélange and not the other possibility, which left the potential for confusion. Memories of the Mars Bar concoction came to mind, and she giggled softly under her breath.

What she saw delighted her—a clever selection of local produce, thoughtfully combined to challenge the palate but not overwhelm it. Starters of local scallops with shallots in a whisky reduction, breast of wood pigeon served on a paté crouton with wild mushroom sauce, and cream of carrot, honey, and ginger soup, all sang to her of the surrounding countryside and everything it had to offer.

The main courses went from good to great. Fillet of Isle of Skye lamb, caramelized apples and pears, with shallots and new potatoes. Slow-cooked blade of Angus beef, with creamed leeks, wild mushrooms, and roasted root vegetables. Roasted Gressingham duckling, with russet potato, chestnuts, and an apple sauce. It was obvious that these guys knew their stuff, and Amy was hungry. This was going to be good.

Finally, the simple dessert selection had her planning her culinary tour de force to ensure that she left enough room to enjoy them, both. It consisted of her absolute favorite, a selection of fragrant Scottish cheeses, served with Kinloch water biscuits, or a baked, rich dark chocolate Fondant with lavender ice cream and warm chocolate sauce.

She settled on the scallops to start, followed by the Isle of Skye lamb then, her digestion willing, a little of the cheese, after the dark chocolate fondant.

As the waiter approached her table, nervously adjusting his white apron, she smiled warmly, trying to put him at ease. Amy ordered her meal and a glass of iced water and, as the waiter walked away, head hunched over his note pad, she noticed three, wide-eyed faces crammed into the small port-hole of the door to the kitchen, staring intently at her.

As she raised her head, they disappeared instantly, and she smiled to herself. If only they knew that she was here because she wanted them to succeed, not to find fault.

Waiting for her first course to arrive, Amy's eyes swept

the dining room, assessing the other customers. To her left, at a small table for two, was an older man, a caricature of a Scottish gent, sporting a muted tweed jacket, and an impressive white moustache. His eyes met hers, and he nodded, almost imperceptibly. He had a large glass of whisky in front of him and, having ordered, was reading a neatly folded broadsheet newspaper, through half-lensed glasses.

Obviously a local, she thought. Amy had long ago outgrown the desire to, out of a sense of solidarity, invite other lone diners to join her. Instead, she nodded back at him and smiled, turning her gaze to the entrance as a young couple walked in. They laughed with the hostess as she guided them past Amy's table to the one next to hers. Nodding their hello's, the couple then turned their attention to the menu.

In the far corner, next to an enormous stone fireplace, sat a family. The parents, and a boy of around ten, spoke softly to each other as the mother indicated something on the menu.

A family friendly eaterie, thought Amy, mentally constructing her article as the evening unfolded.

Three other tables were occupied, one by a group of five, possibly work colleagues grabbing dinner after a long day at the office. The other two by couples, leaving only two tables empty. *Not bad for a Wednesday night,* she thought. *Popular with the locals, Mélange has a lively atmosphere, even on weeknights,* she continued to compose.

Suddenly, the kitchen door swung open as two waiters and a sous chef burst through. There was a loud wailing coming from the kitchen, accompanied by the metallic crash of pots and pans hitting the stone floor.

"Get it. Oh my God, where has it gone?" Someone yelled as a plate went careening into the dining room and slid right under Amy's feet, causing her to jerk them upward so force-fully that her knees smacked the underside of the table.

The boy had sprung up from his seat, and, as his mother reached for his arm to pull him back, he leaned into the entrance to the kitchen and shouted. "There it is. Wow, that's a *really* big mouse."

Amy finished her mental review as, smiling, she rose from the table and made her way to the door. *A delightful bistro in an up and coming neighborhood, and a menu that tantalizes, with promises of fresh, and local, organic perfection. The atmosphere is warm and inviting, and you might be surprised by your culinary experience, with certain unlisted items making a special appearance, on occasion. I'd recommend Mélange, for an all-round entertaining night out. Bon Appetit!*

14

HOMELESS

He had become invisible. As the fact sank in, he mused over the dramatic departure from his status, of not so long ago, the days when he had commanded attention. He would walk into a meeting or a restaurant, and his height and demeanor would communicate that he was taking no prisoners. His time was valuable, more valuable than most of those around him, and he was not to be messed with.

That attitude had emanated from his core, fed by his designer suits, innate confidence in his business acumen and obvious achievements, his physical presence, and an unshakable belief in himself.

How quickly that had changed. He'd often scoffed at the notion that we are all just a few paychecks away from the street, believing that could only happen to lesser individuals than himself—those who were careless, lazy, did not adequately plan ahead, or made bad choices. He'd believed that in some cosmic way, he was immune to those external forces that affected his fellow human beings. His arrogance, and misguided belief that he could defy market forces, and global economics, had buoyed him along far longer than it should. Looking back, he realized that the danger signs had been there long before he'd acknowledged them.

His obsession with success having alienated him from his gentle, artistic brother—the last remaining member of his family—he was now isolated in this new and terrifying reality. For the first time in his life, he was completely alone and vulnerable.

Sitting on the edge of the sidewalk, he nursed a lukewarm coffee that he had retrieved from the garbage outside Starbucks. His tailbone smarted from the pressure of the hard ground as he looked down at his shoes. His once stylish, leather boots had become lumpy, weather-worn extensions of his feet that protruded from the rough linen trousers he'd been wearing when he'd grabbed a few things from the apartment, before being evicted.

As he extended his long legs, pushing his feet out into the street, an empty potato chip packet fluttered by and slapped itself to his thigh. Brushing it away, he wondered if there'd be a bed at the shelter tonight. He wasn't up to fighting for it, so it may be the park for him again.

He noticed that the person who'd abandoned the half-finished coffee had chewed the edges of the cup before replacing the lid, leaving a pattern of tiny dents that he circled his finger around. He wondered about them. *Where did they work, and what did they worry about? Was someone waiting for them at home? What kind of house did they live in?* That cup could have been his less than a year ago. Having had his fill of coffee, he'd have tossed it away, without so much as a thought.

Flinching at the ache in his lower back, he gathered up his rucksack and umbrella. A Gucci umbrella had seemed a frivolous thing to take with him, but he'd been thankful for it, almost daily, since leaving his home.

He turned North, to wade upstream against the tide of workers, headed to their offices.

Interesting concept, poverty, he thought. Truly, the great leveler. The newly flat playing field was a daunting place and, despite all humans having the same basic needs; shelter, water, warmth, and food, there was so much that separated him from those around him.

Hitching his pack higher up onto his shoulder, he walked on, focusing on the traffic lights ahead, avoiding the judgment of passersby. Numerous pairs of eyes slid sideways as he walked past. Earbuds were adjusted, and phones answered, as the crowd split and flowed around him as if Moses had ordered the corporate Red Sea to part, just when he needed it to.

As he reached the crosswalk, he noticed a woman at the opposite side, waiting to cross toward him. She had a small smile tickling her mouth, warm toffee-colored hair, and eyes that were clear and focused. She carried a laptop case, and an umbrella, a duplicate of his own. She looked oddly still, amidst the human river seething around her. The woman absently tucked a strand of hair behind her ear as she watched for the signal to change.

Eventually, she walked toward him, nodding in acknowledgment when their eyes met. Curious, he flicked his head over his shoulder to see where she was looking and realized there was no one directly behind him. She was looking at him. She saw him.

"Nice umbrella," she said, as their shoulders brushed in the middle of the crossing.

He instinctively patted the wooden handle, as it protruded from under his arm. "Nothing but the best," he responded, smiling back at her. He heard a warm laugh floating back to him as she moved on.

The woman continued walking, and he turned to watch her back as it disappeared into the sea of bodies undulating away from him. It was everything he could do to fight the impulse to run after her and grab her arm. *Maybe he could ask her if she wanted to talk some more, or walk somewhere with him?*

With every fiber of his being, he quashed the desire to follow her, and as he turned back toward no specific destination, he found his eyes filling up. Temporary blindness forced him to steer himself to the inner edge of the sidewalk, and to reach for balance against the dark building looming on his left. As he struggled to fill his lungs, he realized that her tiny act of humanity, her simple acknowledgment of his presence, had thrown him a rope. In a split second, that act had made him consider his entire life's journey to this point, making him both grateful and ashamed.

Would he have been that person who had smiled and spoken, or would he have subconsciously moved away from the homeless man, probably assuming the umbrella had been stolen and, despite knowing nothing of their journey, define their life in a nanosecond? His face burned with the certainty that he would have been the latter.

The desire for human interaction overwhelming every other need, his unsteady legs buckled as he leaned back against the gritty face of the building and looked up. Despite the cloud-laden sky of earlier, the day was now bright. The sky, a startling blue, topped the skyscrapers around him, like colored frosting. As he tried to focus on his surroundings, his brother's face materialized before him, and the image of the familiar, warm eyes, the kind smile, drew his throat tight.

When the bottom has fallen out of his world, useless pride

had kept him from reaching out, but finding his brother, his only remaining family, was all that mattered now.

Gathering himself, he hefted his pack onto his shoulder, tucked the umbrella under his arm, and stepped back out into the stream of bodies. This time, he had a very specific destination in mind.

The veil fluttered out of the truck window and fell right at Erin's feet, forming a small puddle of ivory against the grimy sidewalk. Inside the beaten-up vehicle, she could see a woman's white-blonde head, lying against the broad, checked shoulder of the man next to her. He was wearing a dark-colored Stetson, and she leaned into him, their two bodies taking up less than half of the front bench seat.

As the truck pulled away, Erin leaned down and picked up the veil. It was gauzy, and the tiny rhinestones around the edges winked at her in the afternoon sunlight. As she watched the back bumper of the truck bounce away, on an impulse, she shoved the veil into her bag and felt around for her keys, deciding that she would follow the couple.

Her car was close by, and stepping out between two parked vehicles, she crossed the street toward it, scanning the road ahead for the outline of the truck. She felt oddly panicked as the distance between her and the mystery newly-weds increased. They were total strangers to her, and yet, for some unfathomable reason, she had to know where they were going.

The engine turned over, and she pulled out of the space. She could see the rusty tailgate, two cars ahead of her, as it wove deftly through the traffic.

Suddenly her phone chimed, and, at the jarring sound, her heart contracted. No matter how many times she heard the ringtone, she still reacted this way. Her stomach clenched, in the grip of anxiety, as she imagined who could be calling and whether the news delivered would tilt her world on its axis, as it had when the fire chief had called about her husband, Ted.

"Mom? Are you there?" Erin relaxed at the sound of her daughter's voice. Catherine was thirteen and away at art camp. The light of Erin's world, Cat had been vacillating between two states of mind recently, as many teens do, one moment a scathing would-be grown up, and the next a vulnerable child.

"Hi, sweetie. You O.K.?" Erin looked over her shoulder, and crossing the lane, pressed her foot down on the accelerator. In the distance, she could see the truck, its rear light blinking as it sat at the intersection. It was clear that she needed to pick up speed if she didn't want to lose them.

"Where are you?" Cat asked.

"I'm in the car. Is everything all right, Cat?"

"Yeah. I was just bored. You know. Wanted to talk to you." She sighed.

"O.K." Erin frowned. Her daughter rarely called her these days, unless she wanted to be picked up from somewhere. "How come you're bored? I thought you were working on that mosaic project today, with Tiffany?"

"We're done. The plaster's drying. Tiff is in a funk, coz' her loser boyfriend hasn't called, so I'm hanging out in the cabin."

Erin slid into the next lane, and as the two cars in front of her moved away, she found herself directly behind the truck. The two silhouettes inside were still conjoined, at one side of the seat.

"Mom?"

Erin's focus on the truck pulled her forward. This was not her route home, but her car was taking her to wherever the couple was headed. The veil must be returned. It was too precious, too meaningful, to be cast away like a piece of garbage.

"Mom, it's today, isn't it?" Cat tried again.

"Today?" Erin dragged her attention back to her daughter.

"A year. It's a year since Daddy..." Cat's voice faded.

Erin felt a vicious heave under her diaphragm. The sensation of being gutted while awake that she'd experienced almost daily since losing Ted, was just as strong today as 365 days ago.

"Yes, honey. It's today." Suddenly, she remembered her reason for being in town. She had been in the florist buying hydrangeas to take to the cemetery. She'd intended on going straight there from town, then making her way home to take a hot bath. Afterward, she wanted nothing more than to curl up in her overly large and overly empty bed, pull the soft quilt over her head, and will herself to sleep. Sleep was the only way to escape the knives of memory of the day when her life had imploded.

"Are you O.K., Mom?"

"Yes, I'm fine. Are *you* doing alright?" Erin suddenly craved her daughter. She wanted to pull the reluctant teenage body into her arms, and smell vanilla scented hair, feel Cat's bird like ribs through her sweater, and her child's breath on her cheek.

"Yeah. I wish I was home, though." Cat sighed. "Can you come get me?"

Erin watched the truck as it stopped at another intersection, then she pulled up behind it, glancing in the rear-view mirror.

"I could come later this afternoon. But don't you want to stay for the last cookout tonight?"

"Nah. It's lame. Just a bunch of greasy hot dogs, and kids singing kumbaya round the fire. I'd rather be with you."

Erin felt a tug in her middle as she listened to Cat. If she came home, they could eat mounds of ice cream, watch a movie and curl up *together* under the quilt. When tomorrow came, they'd face it, as they had each new day for the past year. United in their loss, theirs was a team of two against the world.

"I'm just running some errands. Do you really want to come home?"

"Yes. Please come get me. I'll be ready by three. And Mom, can we go together, to the cemetery?"

Erin glanced out into the unfamiliar street.

"Yes, of course. I'll wait for you. It wouldn't be the same without you." Erin smiled as she spoke. She could hear her daughter exhale, her relief transmitting itself through the phone.

"O.K., great. You'll have to call my counselor to let her know."

"I can do that. See you soon then."

"I love you, Mom."

"I love you more."

Erin watched the truck pull off the road into a brick driveway. Slowing down, she stopped her car in front of a pretty bungalow. As the woman stepped out of the truck, Erin caught her breath. She had to be in her mid-seventies.

Dressed in a knee-length, cream-colored dress, she carried a small bouquet of hydrangeas, the same blue-ish pink as the ones lying on Erin's passenger seat.

The man held the woman carefully under the elbow as they walked up to the front door. Eric wondered at her surprise at their age. It was an odd reaction, especially as she'd always believed that love knew no boundaries.

Glancing at her bag, she saw the veil trailing out of it onto the seat. The rhinestones, now dull, looked plain to her, cheap. *What was she doing here? If the pale-headed bride had thrown her veil out the window, without so much as a backward glance, what made Erin think she'd want it now?*

Erin let her mind drift back to her wedding day. Ted had worn his dress uniform, and the entire firehouse had turned out to celebrate with them. They'd made it until almost 9.00 pm before the siren sounded, as a call came in. Ted had kissed her, pressed her hand, with the shiny new ring, into his father's palm and said, "Take care of her, Pop. I'll be back."

The thought of Ted's face, ruddy and enthusiastic, the moss-green eyes glinting under his helmet, made her eyes fill up. She needed to go and be with her daughter.

As she drove away from the house, she could see the couple, in the bay window, holding each other close, and Erin smiled through her tears. That was why she was here, why she'd followed them. She just needed to see and believe that there was always hope. And there was.

16

FLORENCE

For only the second time since moving out of the house, Emily was back at the storage unit. She'd been here to locate the title documents for her car, two months before, but hadn't returned since. Being here made her sad, the weight and significance of the contents of the nondescript boxes settling on her like a dark cloud. There were so many reminders, stacked inside the cold concrete cube, that made it hard to breathe.

Shaking the hair out of her eyes, she removed the padlock and pushed the concertina door up above her head. The musty smell made her wrinkle her nose as flipping on the light switch, she scanned the boxes around her, quickly pinpointing the one she was looking for that contained some of her water-color supplies.

With some shoving and twisting, she managed to get the box to the front of the unit and loaded it onto the dolly she'd borrowed from the office upfront then, turning to leave, Emily's hand hovered over the light switch. *Perhaps she'd look through a box or two, just to see if there was anything she wanted to take back to her new apartment?* Lately, she'd begun to feel its modern starkness, swelling with the lack of any personal items.

Scanning the shelves, she walked forward and pulled a smaller box down. Inside, she found a few books on painting techniques and kept two out to take with her. The next box she opened had stacks of old bills, letters, and a bag full of every card or note that her husband Rick had ever given her, since they'd begun dating nine years earlier, starting with the very first Valentine card he'd made from a paper napkin. Seeing it drew her throat into a knot as she re-closed the flaps and exhaled into the chilly room.

Sucked in by nostalgia, she reached for another box. In it, she found all the household account folders, and then photographs, so many photographs stuffed into large brown envelopes—Rick's filing system that had driven her mad with its total lack of any actual system.

Pulling out a stack of envelopes, she lowered herself onto the cold concrete floor. With each one she opened, there, staring her down, were pictorial accounts of Thanksgiving dinners with their families, so many Christmases, vacations, shots of their first home, various before-and-after shots of projects they'd undertaken in the house, and the back yard. Each group of pictures she looked through, then laid out on the floor, took her on another journey jammed with memories, until she was surrounded by images of her life with Rick, her heart thudding dully under her shirt. Looking at the past nine years, fanned out before her, she was suddenly wrung out.

Unable to stop herself, Emily pulled their wedding album onto her lap and opened it. She still loved the ivory dress she'd worn and noticed how the slight tan she'd had, had flattered her. Rick looked so young, and carefree, with a sharp jawline, and sparkling eyes, the eyes that had held her transfixed when they'd first landed on her across her favorite bookshop in Georgetown.

Dragging herself back to the present, Emily flipped the page to another shot, one of her gazing up at him while he looked directly at the camera. Her heart folded over as she remembered how much she'd adored him. He'd been her universe, and she'd willingly tailored her world around him, like a snug wool coat on a windy day. She hadn't resented him for the choices they'd made as a couple. At least she hadn't in the beginning.

As the pages turned, she reflected on the years of their marriage. Rick had always been the more opinionated one, the one who primarily defined their plans and steered their course. If it were to be chicken, or steak for dinner, Italy or Wyoming for their vacation, he'd generally got his way. He'd present the argument, and his logic always seemed sound.

As she flipped through the glossy account of their story-book wedding-day, she wondered when she'd stopped trying to be heard. It wasn't that Rick was cruel, or a bully, he was just so sure of being right that after years in his company, she was as sure of it as he was. She had eventually reached the point where she'd been virtually unable to make a decision without checking with him. He'd say he supported her choices, but, more often than not, he would shake his head and smile at her, like a parent indulging a wayward child, and say 'Sweetheart, I think you know what I think.' leaving her clear that the option she'd selected left much to be desired.

In the early years, she'd just smile back, and shrug her shoulders. Rick would grin and say, 'Aren't you glad you came to your senses and married me?'

They'd both graduated with their Masters' at the same time, she in Art History and he in Finance and Business Administration. They'd always said they'd travel before settling down, maybe even live abroad for a few years before coming home to start a family. They had hit the job trail around the same time and, within weeks of returning from their honeymoon in Maine, while Rick was interviewing with a venture capital firm in Washington D.C., Emily had been stunned to be offered the opportunity of studying in Florence, for a year, with an exchange program organized by one of her professors. Now, as she fingered the photograph in front of her, she remembered how excited she'd been, coming home to their tiny apartment in D.C., bursting to tell Rick, knowing they'd have the year of their lives.

He always said he would support her whatever she wanted to do. He respected her work, and while saying that her painting style was not exactly his taste, he recognized the skill in it. She'd often wondered at him putting it like that and asked him what he'd like to see her paint. Rick had never committed to anything, and so, it had been the one area of her life that had remained pristine, uninfluenced by him. He rarely commented on her works in progress or asked what she was planning for the next piece, and Emily had been puzzled at his apparent lack of interest in her passion.

The delivery of her news about Florence did not go the way she had expected. Rick had met her in the hallway, just having come back from a second interview at the venture capital firm. She knew the minute she saw his face that he had news.

"Baby, you won't believe it," he'd gushed. "I got it." The smile he'd flashed her had almost been bigger than his face could accommodate. "I was up against this older guy with four years of experience, but they still went with me. I killed it, sweetie. We are on our way."

He'd dropped his laptop case inside the apartment

entrance and, as his words tumbled out, grabbed her up into a bear-hug, crushing the air from her lungs.

Her heart had melted with pride as she'd told him how wonderful it was, but, at the same time, a pin had burst her bubble as her momentous news was relegated to second-best, in the blink of an eye.

Later that night, after a celebratory dinner from the Chinese restaurant down the street and a bottle of cheap Chianti, she'd told him her news.

"Oh, wow, Emily, that's amazing," he'd said. "How weird, that we both got great news on the same day?" He'd laughed, re-filling her glass. "Perhaps the opportunity will come up again, sometime?" He'd looked at her closely, waiting for her response.

Emily had been speechless, stricken by the realization that he hadn't considered, for one second, that she might want to at least contemplate this chance to study with a master artist. However, she had simply nodded and taken a huge gulp of the metallic wine.

Finally, finding her voice she'd said, "But what if it doesn't?" She'd scanned his face, waiting for something to hang her hopes on.

"Well, if it doesn't, sweetheart, there will be other things you can do here, right?" Rick had gestured for her to move into his arms, shifting slightly on the sofa to make room for her. "I mean, you wouldn't want to go if I'm here, working in D.C., would you?"

""No, of course not, I just thought maybe we could both go." Her voice had sounded childlike, and petulant, even to herself.

Rick had laughed, and she remembered how she'd heard the blood rushing into her ears, at that point, and her face had been on fire.

""Sweetie, that's nuts." He'd pulled away from her. "I got an offer with a firm that people would kill for. Are you serious?" He was looking at her with wide eyes, and an odd smile twisting his mouth.

"I know. I mean, of course. It's great that you got the job, and I totally support you." She'd said, hating herself for buckling so quickly. "I'm sure there will be other opportunities …" Her voice had become a whisper.

"That's my girl." Rick had scooped her closer into his embrace, and Emily, with a small exhale, had watched Florence float into the ether. His manipulating and her capitulating were to become the pattern of their lives, until now.

She replaced the photographs in the various envelopes, and slipped them into the box, shoving it back against the wall. With the few items that she'd selected, stacked on top of her painting supplies, she maneuvered the dolly out into the icy-cold hallway, flipped off the light, and dragged the heavy door back into place. With the padlock secured again, she turned and put her weight behind the dolly, counting the audible clicks as one of the wheels wobbled dangerously with every turn.

The man in the front office nodded as she approached. "Find everything you needed?" He smiled, his jumble of dark teeth like a row of gravestones under a thick grey mustache.

""Yes, and then some." Emily nodded and then, surprising herself, she blurted, "It's surprising how much of what we keep, we really don't need. Don't you find?" Instantly feeling her face warming, she dropped her gaze to the floor.

The man rolled his eye. "If I had a nickel." He nodded, then turned his attention back to the monitor on his desk.

Emily pressed her lips together and raised her palm in goodbye, as she shoved the dolly toward the door. She'd kept so much she didn't need, for so many years, that the shedding of it was liberating, to the point of making her feel drunk. That headiness, while tinged with flecks of sadness, was driving her on toward her new goals, and now, as the airline ticket to Florence lay comfortably in her purse, she smiled to herself.

Finally, it was her turn.

17

THE GUARDIAN

Harper counted her steps and trailed her fingers along the wall, the familiar bumps in the paint guiding her down her hallway to the front door. As she felt for her jacket, hanging on the coat hook, Jasper's thick coat brushed her calf.

"Come on, boy. Time for your walk." She patted the phone in her jeans and slipped her jacket on, checking the pockets for her extendable cane, and the plastic bags she always carried. Then, she felt along the wall for the door frame. Locating the smooth edge of the wood, she reached down and ran her hand over Jasper's silky head, along his neck to his harness, and lifted the handle. "It's supposed to be lovely out today." She smiled, as she felt the familiar thump of Jasper's tail against her leg. "Oh, you're ready to go, aren't you?" She laughed softly as she felt for the door handle, turned it, and gave the forward command. "On, Jasper."

Out in the corridor, Harper counted the steps to the elevator then traced the cool metal panel on the wall, searching for the call button. Pressing it, she took two steps back and waited as the hydraulic whoosh of the machinery kicked in, the elevator beginning to make its way up to her floor.

The smell of fresh coffee hung in the air, and she breathed it in, almost tasting it, wondering if it was her neighbor, Stephanie, brewing her favorite Kenyan blend this morning. If she heard Harper out in the hallway, Stephanie sometimes popped her head out of her door and invited her in, but there was only silence today.

Harper heard the ping and the elevator doors slide open, so she walked forward the customary four steps, then turned back to face the doors as they swished closed.

As three more pings indicated her progress toward the ground floor, she ran a hand over her long hair, tucking a loose strand behind her ear. She'd washed and straightened it the day before, but the dampness of the previous afternoon had left it deeply waved and kinking under her fingertips.

The doors opened, and as a rush of warm air brushed her face, Harper smelled toast, and something meaty drifting into the lobby from one of the ground-level apartments. Shaking her hair from her face, she walked across the slippery floor, feeling the change from tile to carpet, and back to tile, under her sneakers.

Jasper walked at her side, his flank a guiding force as she moved. Sometimes, she swore she could feel his heart, beating in time with her steps, so close was their connection. He'd been with her eight years now, and she had no idea how she'd managed without him. The transition to working with a guide dog had been easier than she'd imagined, and, when her parents had told her that if she could cope alone, they'd help her buy her own apartment, Harper had enthusiastically taken the classes at the Center for the Blind, in Baltimore, just a few miles from where she now lived, in Fells Point.

Jasper halted and sensing the approaching change in

temperature, Harper extended a hand, reaching for the front door. "On, Jasper." She pulled gently on the harness as Jasper led her through the door and onto the sidewalk.

As the heavy door clicked behind her, the chill of early fall settled on her cheeks, and Harper pulled her collar closed. "It's a chilly one." She felt a gentle tug as the dog moved forward, his strength flowing from his muscular neck up through her arm, and straight to her heart.

Thirty-five steps later, Jasper halted at the crosswalk, and Harper reached to her left for the familiar metal post. Finding it, she ran her fingers across the chilly pole until they found the box with the cross button, which she pressed. A few moments later, they were walking across the cobbled street toward the small park that was their daily haunt. Harper loved to smell the brine of the river to her left and hear the seagulls cawing overhead, as Jasper's pace would pick up the closer they came to the park.

As the texture of the street changed beneath her feet, she waited for Jasper to lean to the right, indicating the entrance to the small patch of green that local residents enjoyed, year-round. In the warmer weather, Harper would sit on the low wall that circled the south end of the space, and listen to children playing, their voices bouncing off the river behind them, filling her ears with notes of joy. She and Jasper had become somewhat of a fixture in the park, at this time of the day, and she enjoyed talking to some of the local regulars and petting their dogs as they passed.

Now, Jasper walked steadily on until she felt the bounce of grass beneath her feet. There was a faint smell of onions in the air, and she turned her face to the right, picturing the food truck that served wonderful breakfast burritos, at the edge of the park. Patting her pocket, she felt the lump of her wallet, and, deciding that she'd treat herself to breakfast, she let Jasper lead her across the grass to the wall.

As he gently guided her to the left, she suddenly felt the harness jolt as he drew her to an abrupt standstill.

"What's up, boy?" She leaned down and patted his side, feeling his heightened breathing under her fingertips. As her heart rate picked up at the shift in his behavior, Harper straightened up and waited.

Jasper was the litmus paper for her environment, her guardian, her eyes. She trusted him implicitly, and if there was something to be concerned about, he'd alert her to it. She would take her cue from him, as she always did. All she had to do was absorb his signals.

Suddenly, Jasper sat down hard, his sign for an obstacle, or hindrance to her progress. Heeding the warning, Harper stood still, listening to the sounds of the morning. Straining to hear if there was anyone around her, she heard a yapping, off to her left.

Jasper panted, his tail swishing back and forth over the grass as Harper smoothed her hair. This kind of thing still made her nervous, and as her anxiety began rising into the back of her throat, she heard the yapping again, closer this time.

As she held her breath, Jasper stood up and pressed himself against her leg, just as two small paws bounced against her right shin. Letting her breath out, Harper leaned down and tentatively felt for the smaller dog, trying to assess who this new visitor was.

"Hello there." She spoke quietly, as her fingers found the soft down of a puppy. Its coat was close and warm, and a cold wet nose brushed her palm. "Hi, cutie." She stroked the little dog as Jasper shifted at her side, his reassuring weight firm against her knee.

"Bob Dylan, come here." A deep voice, alarmingly close to her, startled Harper, and she straightened up. The sudden tension in her arm brought Jasper even closer. "I'm sorry. He's a tyrant." The man's voice was rich and deep, with a drawl that told her he was not from Maryland.

Noting the pup's unusual name, Harper smiled in the direction of the voice. "That's O.K. How old is he?" She held her ground, Jasper, now wedged between her and the stranger.

"Ten weeks." He laughed. "I've aged ten years since I got him, though." The laugh came again, hearty and warm. "Your dog is a handsome guy. May I pet him?"

Harper shook her head. "Best not, while he's working." She dipped her chin toward the harness.

"Oh, of course. That was stupid of me." He sounded contrite, "I'm sorry."

Sensing his embarrassment, Harper took a tentative step forward, Jasper staying close to her leg. "It's fine." She shrugged. "He does get time off from the salt mines, sometimes." She smiled.

She could smell sandalwood and the slight musk of damp wool. "Are you a local?" She reached down and stroked Jasper's head.

"Yes, just moved here, from D.C., a couple of weeks ago." He paused. "You are too, presumably?"

Harper could hear the smile in his voice. "Yes, two years now." She nodded. "I love living here."

"Yeah, it's worked out well for us, hasn't it Bob?"

There was something mellow, and comforting, in the way the man spoke. She pictured him tall, lean, with a broad brow and deep-set eyes. She imagined him leaning down to pet his errant pup when she heard the laugh again.

"Man, you're a pain." At this, the puppy yapped excitedly, and Jasper tensed slightly against the harness.

"So, what brought you to Baltimore?" She shifted her feet, feeling Jasper's paw protectively locking her in place.

"I started a new job here." His breath smelled like fir trees and dew.

"Oh, nice." Harper nodded. "DJ on the radio?" She fought with the smile that tugged at her mouth.

There was a pause, then, the warm laugh floated across her face. "No. Orthopedic surgeon at Johns Hopkins. Why?"

"Bob Dylan." she shrugged, feeling her face warming.

He laughed. "Well, he's a classic." The voice moved closer. "So, what do you do?"

Harper raked her hair from her face. "I work at Hopkins, too."

"Really? Doing what?" He sounded genuinely interested.

"I'm a neurosurgeon." She stared ahead, once again battling with a smile until she could hold it no longer. "No, I'm a braille instructor at the Eye Institute." She laughed softly. "It's an incredible machine that place, isn't it?"

"It certainly is." He brushed her arm with his, and she felt a tingle permeate her jacket. "You're quite the comedienne. What's your name?" He had moved in close to her right side, so Jasper was no longer a buffer, but rather than be nervous about his proximity, Harper relaxed into the space between them.

"Harper, and this is Jasper." She dipped her chin. "And you are?"

"I'm Ben." He was holding the puppy in his arms now, as she could hear the tiny pants close to her eye level.

"Nice to meet you both." The sandalwood smell was now stronger, with his proximity to her side. Bob Dylan yapped again, and in response, Jasper leaned more heavily against her.

"So, Ben, where are you from?" She tipped her head toward him.

"Charleston, originally. You picked up the accent, huh?"

She nodded. "I have a good ear." She patted the side of her head. "Kind of goes with the territory." No sooner had she said it than she sensed him cringing.

"I'm sorry. I didn't mean…" His voice lowered and moved away from her, as she sensed him stepping back.

"Oh, it's no problem." She felt her face warming. "I didn't mean to make you feel bad. It's just a habit, to make jokes about it." She shrugged. "If you can't laugh, right?" She held her breath, hoping that he'd rally, not do what so many did, shifting from friendly to awkward when the elephant in the room became too big to ignore.

Living on her own had been both liberating and terrifying, and while she'd made a friend in Stephanie, and a couple of her co-workers, Harper's life was still quite solitary for the most part. Her blindness seemed to scare people, and that fear created barriers, not of her own making.

"Well, if it's open season, I can play that game." She heard the smile return.

She let out a laugh. "Bring it. I guarantee I'll beat you." She felt Jasper shift, his weight lifting from her leg. He was easing, the tension releasing on the harness, his guarding instincts relaxing as hers did too.

"So, Harper, do you come here often?" Ben chuckled. "Lame line, Ben."

She grinned, picturing him with a wide smile, perhaps dimples appearing at the sides of his mouth.

"Every day, around this time." She nodded. "We're creatures of habit, Jasper and I."

Ben moved in closer to her and, for the first time, she got a sense of his height, as she felt his arm brush hers. "Well, is there somewhere to get good coffee around here?"

She was aware if him bending down and setting Bob Dylan back on the grass.

"There is actually. Right over there." She pointed in the direction of the food truck. "The burritos are killer, too, if you're in the market for breakfast." Suddenly nervous at rashly issuing an invitation to a total stranger, Harper stepped back. "Well, I guess we'd better get going. Jasper needs his walk." She reached down and stroked the silky ears. "Enjoy your morning." She smiled in Ben's direction, hearing him clear his throat.

"Would it be too forward of me to ask you to join me?" He spoke quietly, and the tentative, old-fashioned nature of the question eased her momentary tension. "I won't be offended if you say no."

Feeling Jasper begin to move forward, she smiled. "How about tomorrow?"

"Tomorrow works." Ben was close to her again. "Same time?"

She nodded. "Same time, same place."

"Perfect." He hesitated. "May I shake your hand?"

Startled, Harper hesitated a second or two before extending her hand. His fingers were cool as they wrapped around hers, and her pulse quickened.

"Until tomorrow, then." He pressed his fingertips into her palm before releasing her hand.

"Until tomorrow." She waved as she sensed him moving away, the sandalwood scent fading as he walked in the direction of the food truck.

Jasper stood at her side, his tail swinging slowly, a sign of his relaxed demeanor.

"What do you think, boy? Is he a good one?" She raked her fingers along the dog's side. "One bark for yes and two for no."

Knowing that Jasper seldom barked, and never when he was on duty, Harper jumped when he gave one sharp yap.

"Woah, Jasper. That good, eh?" She laughed as he shifted from foot to foot, his side meeting and leaving her leg. "Got it, sweet boy. I hear you." She pulled her collar up against the breeze that was picking at her face. "Come on, let's walk."

18

THE REUNION

The plane cut through the clouds like a cake-knife through frosting. The mid-morning sky ahead was silvery, with a pink tinge, which reminded Mary of sunrise at the beach near her home in Nantucket.

Right up until the last day, she had been unsure about attending this reunion in Chicago. Thirty years was a long time, and she had kept in touch with only two or three people from her graduating class. She wondered if anyone would recognize the forty-eight-year-old version of herself, and, with that thought, her hand inadvertently went up to her hair, smoothing the fresh and, she hoped, stylish new look.

Mary checked her watch, and adjusted her seatbelt, for the umpteenth time, then glanced back down the aisle, hoping to catch sight of a flight attendant. She was thirsty but too nervous to get up and walk back to the galley to ask for water. The flight had been fairly smooth so far, but you never knew when you might hit unexpected turbulence. As a newly nervous flyer and former flight-staff, she knew better than to wander around mid-flight, unless absolutely necessary.

Deciding that if she couldn't have water right away, she'd

suck on a mint instead, Mary strained against the belt and reached down to retrieve her purse from under the seat in front of her. Bag in hand, she leaned back just as the little boy sitting behind her pushed his feet hard into the seat, yet again, and she felt the pressure on her spine increase. A flash of irritation overtook her, and she turned around sharply, intending on having harsh words with the parents, only to see them both fast asleep either side of the child. The mother's head was tipped at an awkward angle against the window, a coat bunched under her cheek, cushioning her face from the cloudy plastic. The father was leaning back against a pillow, his mouth gaping. Mary saw his cheeks fluttering slightly, with each exhale, and thanked heaven for the ambient noise of flying, as otherwise she'd have been subjected not only to the pummeling she was receiving but also to the joy of hearing the man's snores.

The little boy looked approximately five or six and, with earphones in, was transfixed to the miniature TV screen in front of him. His expression was rapt, and seeing it, Mary's anger dissipated. His big brown eyes followed what she guessed was an animated character around the screen, and a smile played on his mouth.

Giving up the notion that she'd make much of an impression, she patted the back of her seat and shook her head at him, hoping that at least a modicum of her message would permeate. The boy did not take his eyes from the screen, and Mary, realizing the futility of her situation, turned back toward her own monitor.

The passenger next to her was working on his laptop and, to Mary's relief, wasn't a talker. They'd exchanged pleasantries, right after take-off, but since then had settled into a companionable silence.

Looking back down the aisle, there was still no sign of an

attendant, and Mary smiled to herself, recalling when she had worked with the airlines. It had been a great way to save for law school, and those three years had changed her, opened her eyes and mind to the world outside her little microcosm, in Massachusetts.

They'd been known as stewardesses in her day, and they'd commanded a great deal of respect. The dark blue uniforms had carried with them a certain mystique, and she'd always felt special, walking through airport complexes, inside the elite group of women in their smart suits and black high heels, dragging their little travel-bags with tiny pillbox hats pinned to their heads. They had all been aware of the stares as they bypassed security, such as it was then, and having reached their destination and cleared customs, would turn as one, as a flock of birds might, toward the new city that would be their home for the night. In those days, she'd worn her hair twisted up into a chic roll and had favored ruby-red lipstick. Now she hated lipstick and wouldn't have lasted five minutes in those heels, but that was then, and this was now.

The little feet behind her shoved her mid-section forward again, and Mary, resigned to the annoyance, rifled in her purse for her book. Thirty more minutes and she'd been in Chicago. Pulling the dog-eared paperback out, she wondered if she'd recognize Andrea. After the invitation to the reunion had come out, they'd begun emailing each other, and had figured out that they would be arriving into Chicago at approximately the same time. They had arranged to meet in the airport and travel out to the hotel together. Andrea had been in drama club with Mary, and while they had never been particularly close friends, they had gotten along well enough.

High school had been O.K. Not her best years, but far from the nightmare it had been for some. Mary had kept mostly to herself and had survived it. Meeting Chuck had been the highlight, and now, thirty years later, they were still together. Thinking of him brought a prickle of pain, as her disappointment at his absence renewed itself. He had been registered for a medical conference in L.A. for months when the notice about the reunion had arrived. She'd hoped he would find a way to wriggle out of the conference, but when she'd asked him about it, he'd smiled and said there was no way he could.

She recalled his amused expression as he'd quipped, "I am the keynote speaker on embryonic cryo-preservation sweetheart, so the chances are, I'll probably be missed."

She sighed as she thought about her husband, and her customary pride in him brought a smile to her face. How many couples he had helped realize their dreams of having children when all other options were closed to them. She'd lost count. So, she'd be alone at the reunion and had brought some photos of them together, should anyone ask about him. After all, she wanted to prove to the naysayers that they were still together after all these years. Yes, the quiet, mousey girl from drama group had become a respected attorney, had married the golden-haired Chuck, class president and straight-A student, who half the school had idolized for his good looks and kind manner. Twenty-nine years of marriage and they still adored one another, that in itself was worth celebrating, and even if she felt a little self-satisfied, Mary believed she was justified in a slight sense of achievement.

Her ears filled with pressure as the plane banked to the left, and the captain's voice came over the PA system, announcing that they'd begun their descent. Mary felt her stomach quiver at the familiar sensation of losing height, and, coupled with her general nerves at the event ahead of her, she wriggled in her seat.

Her neighbor closed his laptop and slid it under the seat.

Groping for his seat belt, the young man's hand grazed Mary's thigh, and she jumped slightly at the unexpected physical contact.

"Sorry, ma'am." He blushed and shrugged, as Mary reached down the side of her seat, retrieved the errant strap and handed it to him.

"That's O.K," she said. "It happens."

The clouds thinned and she saw the ground begin to materialize beneath them. Landing was her least favorite part of flying, these days. As the plane heaved upwards slightly, catching a pocket of warm air, she gripped the armrest then tightened her seatbelt one more time, for good luck.

She was nearly there. She'd almost done it. She'd taken herself out of her comfort zone, flown on her own again, after years of choosing land-based travel, left the moral support of her husband behind, and was ready to face the doubters and critics of her youth. Her hair was in place, her favorite red dress lay in tissue paper inside her suitcase, and her photos were snuggly tucked into her purse. She could do this, so bring it on McAllister High. Bring it on.

My name is Isabella, but my family called me Isa. I was sixty-nine, on March 15th, 1983, when my body was catapulted into the air as I was hit by a taxi, traveling at around 30 mph.

I had been rushing through the rainy night to my local corner store. My daughter and her family were coming to visit, and I was making a batch of toffee for my grandchildren when I ran out of sugar.

A neighbor reached out a friendly hand to stop me from stepping out from behind the parked car.

"Don't go yet, Mrs. MacKenzie."

I heard him clearly, but in my haste, I was sure there was plenty of time.

Later that night, the doctors would tell my children that my thick sheepskin coat had kept me from dying instantly, protecting me somewhat from the impact of the vehicle.

I watched as the ambulance pulled away from the road-side, lights flashing and sirens blaring. I reached instinctively for my collar; an age-old Scottish superstition, supposed to help one ward off a similar fate to that of the occupant. I didn't have a collar anymore, and I couldn't feel my hands, or face, or clothes.

My heart stopped beating in the ambulance on the way to the hospital. My body tried to keep up with my soul, but the conscientious paramedics revived me, dragging me back from blessed obscurity. The pain in my head was overwhelming, and I felt the broken bones in my legs and pelvis grind as they moved me out of the ambulance and into the hospital.

My body lingered shallowly in that hospital bed, for a year, after the accident, my head fuzzy and my spirit confused. People I loved came and went from my bedside and the shadows of my consciousness. Sometimes it was easy to remember them all, and other days, the faces began to merge.

I was being pulled backward, trying to swim against the strong under-current tugging at me. Memories of my children building sandcastles, wrapping Christmas presents, and throwing snowballs at each other were floating around me. Part of me wanted so much to be with them again, immersed in their lives, and part of me wanted to go home and join my Jack, who'd gone on before me many years before.

Jack came and sat by me, almost every day, throughout that year. We left my broken body in the bed and went traveling together. We visited my granddaughter working in Europe, and my daughter and her family living in the Far East. I'd always wanted to see Rome and Moscow, and he showed them to me then.

It was frustrating when I heard myself referred to as lucky to be alive when I knew my soul was being wrenched back into an irreparable shell that was preventing me from moving on. I lay limp and thinning in the dry, hot room, my skin becoming more translucent every day as my shaved hair slowly grew back from the site of the surgery I'd undergone, to remove the blood clots from my brain.

I ached to comfort my children and grandchildren, who came unfailingly to my bedside and whispered for me not to leave them. Though silent, I was there, through every visit, every moment, through every one of their thoughts and prayers, watching from the shadows. The incredible force of their combined love and pain kept me from leaving. I had been blessed, with such a wealth of devotion from my family, that it surrounded me, paralyzing me, more than the broken body ever could.

It's just a body, I wanted to whisper. *Don't mourn that. It's not where I am, or who I am.*

Finally, the day came when I was so close to peace that I couldn't bring myself to go back inside the pain and open my eyes for them. It was enough.

I was aware of one of my sons sitting at my bedside, holding my hand, as a single tear made its way down his cheek and lingered under his jaw.

I'm here, John. It's not frightening. I spoke to him and stroked his thinning hair with an invisible hand, while my useless flesh lay heavy on the bedcover. But his pain blocked my message, and I was unable to comfort him.

I wish I'd been able to reassure him, to make him understand that there was nothing to fear in the darkness; in obscurity. There was warmth, familiar souls, peace and best of all, my Jack, all waiting for me.

How could I make John see that this was not a journey fraught with fear, but one that I now craved? I stroked his face, with the shadow of a hand I didn't recognize, and then, one year to the day that I was making that toffee, I finally went home to Jack.

20

TAXI

My stomach lurches as the plane moves into the queue for takeoff. There's nothing sedate about this movement, and I feel the tension creep, like noxious ivy, up from my shoulders to my face, making me grimace.

"Are you O.K.?" Alec asks me.

"Seriously?" I snap back. Then reach for his hand, instantly regretting my tone. *Why didn't I take my sister up on her offer of a Valium? Stupid pride. Next time, for sure, if I survive this.*

The captain instructs the cabin crew to prepare for take-off. I'm aware of the clamminess forming between mine and Alec's hands. I squeeze his fingers, and smile weakly at him, hoping for some form of reprieve.

We don't *have* to go. I visualize us sliding out from our seats and beating a path to the emergency exit, lifting the forbidden lever and leaping from the gaping door as the plane begins to taxi toward the runway. *Would our ankles break from the impact of the fall?* Even if they did, it'd be worth it.

Snapping me back to reality, the plane jolts, and begins creeping toward the runway. The noxious smells, of fabric, sweat, fast food and fear, meld with the tepid air that hits my face as the air conditioning kicks in.

We settle back in our seats, and watch the dark landscape begin to move past our grimy porthole, first slowly, then gradually faster and faster. My throat tightens as we bounce onward, and I'm swallowing over something that feels like a walnut. This feels like starting a ten-year sentence for something I didn't do. I'm trapped, sick to my stomach and angry, all at once.

Is there enough runway? Why isn't the nose going up? Does this guy know what he's doing? Just my luck, a rookie pilot having a bad day.

Suddenly the nose lifts and then comes the dreaded heaving lurch upward as the bulk of the plane becomes supported only by air and prayer.

Just breathe. With no hope of parole or time off for good behavior, I need to keep my head down and focus on the endpoint. I visualize my release into the most welcome fresh air in memory and imagine the glorious comfort of terra firma, coming up to meet my hot, swollen feet. I try tasting the euphoria of having made it, one more time, which will envelop me and give me a sense of invincibility. I'll walk smugly through the airport looking nonchalant and bored as we weave our way through passport control. Once through customs, we'll join the throng all heading toward the many exits, ready for the next stage of our journey.

We'll descend into the bowels of Heathrow airport, tired, relieved and ready, to face the next challenge on the way to the family reunion we're heading to. We'll see the line forming ahead of us as the rain pounds onto the grey tarmac outside the terminal. Pushing our way along, with heavy bags in tow, anxiety will begin to take hold as we tumble out onto the sidewalk, looking for that elusive nugget of gold at the end of this particular rainbow—a taxi.

There was nothing remotely sensible about this dress. It hung, no, floated on the hanger, in an ethereal cloud of impracticality, and Felicity was snared. The material, silk chiffon, the color, a violent red, this garment was everything she hated about women's clothing. The low front was cut low, to enhance, or, more accurately, draw attention. The skirt was a little too short, and the dress being sleeveless (not advisable after a certain age) made it all the more maddening. It was also extremely expensive.

She let the feather-light material slide over her hand. *How could something so insubstantial, cost so much? Where on earth would she wear this?*

A sales assistant, who'd been lurking nearby approached, and Felicity felt her hackles go up at the woman's proximity. *Why couldn't she be left to browse in peace?*

"Can I help you find something?"

"No." Felicity snapped, then, embarrassed by her rudeness, added, "Thanks, but I'm fine."

The woman, who had looked stung by Felicity's tone, regrouped and nodded at the red dress. "It's gorgeous, isn't it?"

All Felicity wanted was to be left to ponder, wander about and kill some time before her meeting. Seeing the attorney who was executing her father's Will was not something she relished the thought of, his death still being so fresh. *How could he have gone and left her here, alone?* He'd been all the family she had left.

"Can I get it in your size?" The woman tried again.

"No. Really. I'm just browsing."

Felicity let the soft fabric drop. Embarrassed by the rush of emotion, the thought of her father had provoked, she turned her back to hide her pink face.

"Well, let me know if there's anything I can help you with." The saleswoman spoke to Felicity's back, until, finally, surrendering to Felicity's mumbled thank you, the woman walked away.

Felicity glanced at her watch. She had another forty-five minutes until her meeting. There had been no point going back to the office after her morning interview was over, and the idea of having this sliver of time to herself had seemed attractive. Now, she hated how alone she felt and wished she'd made the trek back to work, after all, just to be surrounded by the people, noise, and activity of the news-paper editing room.

She circled the store, sliding hangers along silver rails, holding out silken arms and well-cut trouser legs as she went. She wasn't really in the market for anything specific, but having nothing else to do, she went on looking.

The large latte she'd drunk lay heavy in her otherwise empty stomach. In the week since her dad had died, she'd been unable to eat much. Her throat felt permanently constricted, and her stomach had rebelled against anything she had managed to swallow.

As she passed a full length 'make-you-look-skinny'

mirror, Felicity caught sight of her reflection. Her chestnut-colored hair was tousled, dark shadows cupped her eyes, and her silver-grey suit and white shirt looked suitably stern. Her trousers were slightly looser on her than usual and, fleetingly, she wondered how much weight she'd lost.

The idea that she could perhaps fit into a smaller size now, thanks to her dad's untimely demise, brought an incongruous lift to her trampled spirits. She smiled to herself, hearing her father's voice reminding her that there was usually a silver lining if you looked hard enough. "Even where you'd least expect it," he'd say.

She walked purposefully back to the red dress. There were three of them hanging together, so she pulled her size from the rail, and then hesitated. *Perhaps she'd try the size down?*

Inside the small cubicle, she slipped the dress over her head. It slid across her shoulders in a silken caress and, to her surprise, cascaded smoothly over her hips. No resistance, no struggle, it settled on her body like chiffon rain, coating her in its vibrant redness. The zip went up easily, and Felicity lifted her head to see her reflection. The black socks, hanging loosely around her ankles, did nothing for the overall image, so she stepped on the toe of one, then the other, sliding her feet out of them.

Now, with the full length of her legs and feet exposed, she smiled. *Damn this felt good. Like having chocolate soufflé for breakfast.* Overwhelmed by the sense of indulgence the dress evoked, tears pricked her eyes again. *What was she thinking?* She was going to hear her father's Will read. This thing was totally inappropriate, *and* it cost close to two week's wages.

As she pulled the dress up over her head, Felicity felt the soft fabric whisper as it passed her ears. *I fit you perfectly. I am here, especially for you. You deserve me after the week you've had. And, your dad loved red.*

She put her sensible reporter suit back on and lifted her purse. The dress hung inside out on the wall hook, like a limp red skin she'd just shed. Its power had been somehow diminished by the lack of hanger to hold the shoulders out, and the newly exposed lining, less lush than the outer fabric, cheapened it somehow.

Undeterred, Felicity gathered it up and walked out into the store.

The saleswoman smiled as she approached the register. "Oh, so you decided to get it, then?"

"Yes. What the heck, right?" Felicity shrugged.

"Well, good for you. We all deserve a little treat now and then."

"You're right. We do."

As the woman started to fold and wrap the dress in soft white tissue paper, Felicity held her palm out. "Hang on. I think I'll wear it."

The saleswoman quickly scanned her for any signs of humor, but Felicity's face was smooth, expressionless.

"Oh, right."

Felicity handed over her credit card, and, picking up the dress and her receipt, she walked back to the fitting room.

With the dress back on, she dragged a brush through her tangled hair, swiped on some nude lipstick and slid her bare feet into her black pumps. A few moments later, she emerged, the dress clinging to her and her grey suit inside the store's garment bag.

As she passed the skinny mirror again, she nodded, taking in the uncharacteristic boldness of her reflection. She *never* did anything like this, just on a whim. Lifting her two fingers to her forehead, she saluted. *This is for you, Dad.*

ACKNOWLEDGMENTS

My sincere thanks to everyone who came out to play with me on this little book, specifically to Peggy Lampman, my friend and fellow author, for her wisdom and invaluable support.

To my husband. I am beyond grateful for his love, support and unwavering belief in me, every single day. Somewhere in my youth, or childhood...

Heartfelt thanks to Carly Guy and Lesley Shearer, my staunch allies, sage advisors, and the best sisters anyone could ask for.

A huge thank you to all the friends, readers, reviewers, book-bloggers, my wonderful ARC crew and members of my Highlanders Club, who support me, specifically Susan Peterson of Sue's Booking Agency, Linda Levak Zagon of Linda's Book Obsession, Tonni Callan and Kristy Barrett of A Novel Bee, Denise Birt of Wild Sage Blog, the Novels and Latte Bookclub, Annie Horsky McDonnell and Serena Soape of The Write Review, Samantha Alvarez, and Janelle Madison of Green Gables Book Reviews. Thanks also to

Chloe Jordan, Bambi Rathman, Tina Hottinger, Pam Vogt, Lori Beam, Jackie Shephard, Sue Baker, Kay Enderlin, Linda Keenan, Robin Batterson, JoDena Pysher, Linda Smith, Tammy Meadal Underhill and all the wonderful Instagram bloggers on the book tour: @katerocklitchick, @arireadsitall, @notinjersey, @bookstilbedtime, @thebookclubmom, @what_kel_reads, @Cindyroesel_readsandwrites, @beautifulbookmama, @SamAlvarez823, @carol_doscher_reader, @yaaas_or_nahs_books, @Donnamartinreads, @novelsnlatte, @candidwithcourtney, @abduliacoffeebookaddict23, @jypsylynn, @read_by_red, @3heartsandawish, @BooksBeautyandOtherBits, @Catherine.poe.reads, @bibliolau19, @nature.books.and.coffee, @nikkiwilhelm04, @readinggirlreviews, @Tina_readsbooks, @the.bookishworld.of.yrralh, @Nurse_bookie, @BookCrazyBlogger, @shobizreads, @readwithjillandjune, @theweekendbooker and @read-247_instyle_inca. Every one of you made the journey more enjoyable.

A special thank you to Kate Rock, for her smarts and fabulous promotional skills.

If I haven't named you, it's not because I don't appreciate you, so I'll say another sincere thank you to all those not mentioned individually. I couldn't do this without you.

ABOUT THE AUTHOR

Originally from Edinburgh, Alison now lives near Washington D.C. with her husband and dog. A former professional dancer, and marketing executive, Alison was educated in England and holds an MBA from Leicester University.

The Liar and other stories is Alison's sixth book. For more information on upcoming projects go to www.alisonragsdale.com.